TRAFFIK GAMES

Carol K Howell and Sheila Hollihan-Elliot

Palm Beach Press

Golem Bookworks
Engender Bookworks
Palette Bookworks
divisions of
Palm Beach Press Inc

ISBN-13: 9794806124013 softcover

ISBN-13: 9798828551743 hardcover

Library of Congress Control Number: 2022939553

Cover design by: Sheila Elliot and Daniel Goldberg

Printed in the United States of America

Imprint: Engender Bookworks for

Palm Beach Press, Inc.
PO Box 531
Palm Beach, Fl, USA
33480

CONTENTS

PROLOGUE

Jadali Desert, 1994

As soon as the ugly stranger asked her brother whether she bled, Najima took off. No one was around except for some old men cracking watermelon seeds between their teeth and women baking flatbread under the coals. Everyone else was out with the herds, as she would be if the stranger hadn't come to call. Her older brother, Ghassan—absolute ruler of the family now that her father was dead—had welcomed him as an honored guest, saying *Ahlan wa Sahlan*, rest as in your home. And he had ordered Najima, not her mother, to bring refreshments. That was not a good sign.

After helping prepare the tray of guest food—spicy lamb pastries, dates and cheese, hot cardamom coffee—Najima tugged her headscarf down to her eyebrows and carried the tray past the hanging carpet that separated the men's side of the tent from the women's. Zainab tried to come with her, but Ghassan impatiently waved their mother back. Eight-year-old Abdullah—Abdi—reclined on a cushion as if he were a little sultan. Ghassan had not dismissed *him*. What's more, Abdi was pretending to read a newspaper Ghassan had brought back from the city when they all knew he wouldn't learn to read until he went away to school next year. Was he trying to impress their guest?

Najima knew Zainab hoped the stranger was here to arrange a potential match—her one fervent wish was to marry her daughter off—but Najima could tell his purpose was not so honorable. It was the way he looked at her when she brought the tray. Something oily in his gaze. Instead of keeping her eyes lowered, she watched him scan her body, up and down, as if trying to discern the shape beneath her loose black *madraga.*

"*As-salaam alaikum, fatat,*" he greeted her finally.

Najima heard the subtle sarcasm. He was calling her "young lady," but he didn't mean it.

Ghassan nudged her and she mumbled the response: "*Walaikum-asalaam.*"

The stranger smiled. "How old?" he asked Ghassan.

"Thirteen," her brother replied.

"And has she bled yet?"

That was when Najima banged down the tray and fled the tent despite her brother's hiss of disapproval. It didn't matter. Ghassan always disapproved: Najima was too bold, too argumentative, too independent, always racing off like a child even though she was now of marriageable age. And Zainab might pray as hard as she could for a wedding, but Najima knew —because Ghassan had told her, in disgust, many times—that none of their clan or even the tribe would be willing to pay a bride-price for her. She was rebellious: it would be asking for trouble.

She raced past the strange Land Rover—a big ugly box with enormous wheels that could run on sand. Yanking her headscarf off and hiking up her *madraga,* she ran past the old men, the goat-hair tents, the dry *wadi* that would soon fill with water and burst with grass and flowers: yellow, purple, red. But now, like everything else, it was still dusty earth. Barefoot, she ran for the mountain, veering away from the goats grazing on tough shrubs, the girls tying sticks of kindling to their backs. Just yesterday she'd been one of them, worried about nothing more than vipers, scorpions, and packs of wild dogs.

The stranger was a wild dog disguised as human. Most likely he was a *sheytun,* a devil: she had seen his eyes as they traveled her body. She'd heard him tell Ghassan that she would go to live with a wealthy city family—*ya salam*, ten chandeliers in the big house alone!—that she would be fed, clothed, protected, and even paid, a salary sent home to her family while she learned modern domestic skills. He might as well say she was going to be a *houri* and fly straight to Paradise. Every word that fell from his lips was a lie.

She climbed far enough to see beyond the mountain to the desert, a sea of sand and light so harsh it reduced the world to two dimensions. If the stranger took her away, she wouldn't be here when the rains came, and the *wadi* bloomed. She wouldn't be here to help her mother gather leaves and roots to make medicines. She wouldn't be here when everyone wrapped themselves in wet sheets to get cool enough to sleep. And when —*if*—she came back? Would the tribe still be here, or would they have moved on? And if they moved, how would she find them again?

There. This was the place she'd been seeking. All but hidden among the rocks and scraggly juniper trees: the tumbled remains of a goddess. Whenever the tribe returned to the mountain, Najima's mother brought her here, always in secret, for recognizing other gods was blasphemy, expressly forbidden in The Judgments. The great chunks of pocked stone—once head and swollen breasts and bulging belly—had settled deeper into the sandy earth. Zainab had always brought flowers to scatter over the ruins, but nothing was in bloom now. Najima broke a twig from a shrub, one with a little green attached, and laid it across the goddess's rounded belly. She was a very old goddess, worshiped by nomads long before The Judgments were revealed. A fertility goddess.

Zainab would always close her eyes and speak silently, raising her clasped hands, beseeching. But before Abdi, she'd had three stillbirths, one after another. All girls. Najima's sisters. Buried now in the desert with no graves to visit, no place to mourn and wail against injustice, for, as Baba had said, who are we to question God's will? And besides, Ghassan had added in Najima's ear, some animal would surely dig up the bodies and devour them, for did not the desert need to replenish itself? This too was God's will.

Zainab, Najima, and the women of the tribe dug the hole each time and buried the tiny body. No man attended, not even Baba, not for a girl. After the third stillbirth, Zainab stopped her visits to the goddess.

"Ya Na*jeee*mah!" The sound carried in the still air. It was Abdi, trudging up the mountain to find her.

Najima hastened to intercept him—he must not be allowed to see the remains of the goddess: he would blab instantly to Ghassan and all the tribal elders.

"Najima!" Spotting her, he stopped and folded his arms. "Ghassan wants you."

"Why?"

Abdi scowled, doing his best to imitate their formidable brother despite his pudgy cheeks and belly. "Come and you'll see."

As she caught up with him, Abdi stopped and gestured, like Ghassan dismissing their mother. "Behind me!"

"Don't be ridiculous—you're an infant."

"I am not! Next year I go away to *school,* but you don't! And females always walk behind males. Ghassan says so!"

"Do The Judgments say so?"

Abdi scowled even harder, which made him look as if he had a terrible bellyache. "The Judgments say women should dress *modestly.*" He looked pointedly at her bare head.

Najima gave in and tugged on her scarf. Yesterday she would have plopped herself down and refused to follow an eight-year-old trying to give her orders. But yesterday the stranger had not come, talking of cities, chandeliers, and salaries. No point in making Ghassan any angrier.

Zainab was waiting outside the tent with the men, wearing her plainest black *abaya.* It dropped from the top of her head to the ground, leaving holes around the eyes, but Najima could see sorrow in her mother's slumped shoulders. Zainab was holding Najima's *abaya* and a small bundle, probably clothing and the cloth strips for her monthly blood. That meant she was indeed leaving.

"*Mabrook*, little sister!" Ghassan congratulated her, getting to his feet. "You have just contributed to the family."

So, she was right: the stranger was a slave-trader, a merchant who dealt in human beings instead of livestock. Her brother had sold her.

She tried to hold his gaze. "Ghassan?"

He held up both hands. "It is decided."

Zainab stepped forward with Najima's *abaya*, the bundle of clothes, and some flatbread, pressing them into her daughter's hands. Najima resolved at that moment to show no weakness or fear.

Once she was covered from head to toe, the trader spoke, gazing boldly at her face as if he could see through the cloth. "Now you will live in a big, beautiful house with marble floors, sinks with gold handles, beds made of ostrich feathers."

"Ostrich feathers!" Abdi cried, hopping in excitement.

"*Haqana?*" said Najima. "Oh, really? And will *I* be the one sleeping on ostrich feathers?"

The trader's ugly face cracked a grin. "She's smart," he told Ghassan. "She'll do well if she can learn to hold her tongue."

"I *am* smart," Najima retorted. "I could go to school just like Abdi." She did not add that her mother had already taught her to read and write just as her own mother had taught her. The women in their family taught their daughters, but in secret.

"You know what they say." The trader held up a finger to quote the proverb: "*Educating a woman is like letting the nose of the camel into the tent: eventually it will edge in and take up all the room.*"

The men laughed and shook hands.

"I'll give you a moment to say goodbye," the trader said and climbed into his Land Rover.

Abdi, forgetting his superiority, threw his arms around his big sister. Perhaps he would miss her after all. But he disappeared into the tent without a backward glance.

Ghassan gripped her shoulder. "Conduct yourself properly," he said in an even sterner voice than usual. "Remember, your honor is not yours alone: it belongs to the family." He took firm hold of her chin. "If you stain our honor, it is my duty to cleanse the stain. Do you understand?"

Najima looked at him in his white *thobe* and *ghutra*, easily picturing a rifle slung over his back. She nodded. As he swung away, she heard the clink of coins beneath his robes.

Then there was only Zainab, her eyes overflowing. Najima knew that her mother was thinking of the wedding her only living daughter would never have: no elaborately embroidered wedding dress, no veil of golden coins, no intricate henna designs painted on her hands and feet, no roasted camel stuffed with roasted sheep, no sword dance by the men, no *zaghruut*—women ululating, competing to see who could be shrillest and loudest.

"*Uma*," Najima said. Her face was wet too. They clutched each other as hard as they could, hard enough to last a lifetime. Her mother tried to speak but couldn't. They looked at each other one last time through their veils.

"*Yallah!*" called the trader from his Land Rover. "Let's go!"

"*Allah ya selmek*," Zainab choked out. "God protect you, my daughter."

Despite her resolve to be strong, and the trader's fingers drumming on the steering wheel, Najima cracked just for a moment and clutched her mother again.

"*Uma!*" she cried. "Don't send me away!"

Zainab only wept harder. There was nothing she could do. They both knew that.

Then the trader blasted his horn so long that Najima tore herself away, fearing Ghassan would rush back out. She heaved herself up, climbing onto the back seat of the monstrous machine. The passenger windows were painted black except for a small patch in the center, through which she could just see her mother as they pulled away. Najima said a silent goodbye to the goddess, to the goats, to her lost sisters out in the desert. Then, drying her face with her *abaya*, she faced front. Despite her grief, she could not quite ignore the fizzy sensation, a tingling just below her ribcage, something like *excitement.* She was going beyond the camp, beyond the mountain, beyond the desert into the great world. School or not, she would see, and she would learn. *Inshallah.* If it was God's will.

In the loud ugly truck, Najima watched as miles of pure sand speeding past gradually turned to gravel strewn with trash, and scraggly trees were replaced with oil derricks, eyes straining for her first glimpse of the great city rising up on the horizon, glittering in the sun like the fearsome palace of the *djinn.*

CHAPTER ONE

London, 1996

"Dear God! Are they royalty? Do I curtsy?"

Celeste was only half-joking as their driver joined the long line of limousines hauling exquisitely dressed guests to the grand opening of the new Farouqi mansion—a startling white palace occupying a full city block, surrounded by high walls like any Jadali compound. The process slowed even more as security guards checked invitations and peered into each car as it passed—no joke, especially after the recent I.R.A. bombings.

"They're not royalty, and even if they were, you wouldn't curtsy," said her ex-husband. "You're an American, not a citizen of Jadal."

"Are Jadali women citizens of Jadal?"

"Don't ask that question inside."

Celeste reached over to pat Neil's cheek. His tendency to take everything literally was one of the things she didn't miss about their marriage. That was Willow's problem now—Willow the former supermodel wife that Celeste and her loyal girlfriends had tried their best to hate. But that had turned out to be difficult: yes, Willow was tall and beautiful, but she was also warm and friendly, and she'd given Neil the child that Celeste had been unable to conceive—the reason for their amicable divorce. And who couldn't admire the fabulously successful cosmetics empire she'd built, named *Willow*, of course, which she was constantly traveling to expand world-wide? In fact, Celeste had dropped her off at the private airport just this morning—they enjoyed exchanging what Celeste called Neily Notes—and hugged her goodbye. Willow was a dear, even if Maxwell, the two-year-old son-and-heir Neil had longed for, spent most of his time with his nanny, something which confounded Celeste: if she'd ever been lucky enough to get pregnant, she was damn sure no one would have mothered that child but her.

But Willow had a business to run, and she was in—Denmark? —tonight, so Celeste stepped in as usual to take her place. Was it odd to be your ex-husband's date? No matter. The Brits considered all Americans odd, and not in a lovable eccentric way.

"Now Celeste," Neil began in the tone that meant he was about to lecture. "You haven't socialized with Jadalis before, so I thought there might be a few things—"

"Just tell me, Neil."

"All right. Don't extend your hand to the sheik. And don't touch his wives unless they touch you first."

"They?"

"There are two of them."

"Why didn't you think of that, Neil? You could've saved a bundle on alimony."

"That's exactly the sort of thing you shouldn't say tonight. Don't make jokes about their culture or say anything that could be interpreted as a joke."

"Goodness."

"Don't eat or drink with your left hand—"

"What? Surely, they don't do *that* anymore."

Neil shifted, uncomfortable. "No, of course not, they use toilet paper like everybody else. But it's still considered impolite, if not taboo. Don't prolong eye contact with any of the men. Don't—"

"What about winking? Is winking allowed?"

"Celeste, can you not be a smart-ass just this once?"

"Just this once? I can be a smart-ass the rest of the time?"

Neil heaved a sigh.

Celeste relented. "Don't worry, I won't embarrass you. I know this is a big deal."

"It literally *is* a big deal. The sheik—Muhktar Farouqi—and his son Tariq are the richest Jadalis next to the royal family. They made their fortune not just from oil but also construction: urban development, malls, hotels. Now they want to install new plastic piping—it doesn't get as hot as metal—and Ted and Richard and I—"

"I know. You've cornered the market on plastic pipes."

"Well, not *cornered*. There are competing bids."

Neil was being humble. When Margaret Thatcher privatized Britain, he and his partners had made a fortune for themselves and their clients, buying up oil and gas, electricity, water, steel, making those stodgy enterprises wildly efficient and profitable. So, a contract for plastic pipe manufacture—which could spread from Jadal throughout the Middle East—would be a very big feather in their cap.

A candy-apple red Lamborghini abandoned near the top of the drive forced limos to pull around, but they'd inched far enough for Celeste to get a look at the new house. It was definitely a palace, hulking and enormous, brand-new but built to look old. In front, a ring of rearing stone stallions surrounded a glittering fountain tiled in turquoise and gold. Unfortunately, she couldn't see more due to the throng of journalists blocking the way.

"How nice," she said flatly. "The press."

"Some of them aren't so bad. Willow knows everybody." Neil stepped out of the car as a security guard opened the door. "Hello, Rhys!" he called to one reporter. The cameras flashed in his direction. "How are you, mate? Hello Sandra, Nigel!"

Show-off. Before she followed him, Celeste leaned forward to speak to their driver, Benny. She was very fond of Benny—he was married to her Filipina housekeeper Flora, and God knew she couldn't survive without Flora. They lived in the apartment above her garage, which was not only convenient but reassuring.

"Don't go *far*, Benny," she told him. "This might be an early night. Got your phone?"

He grinned, holding up the brand-new Motorola that matched hers. Though chunky and hard to stuff in her evening bag, it was still the smallest and lightest on the market. They had practiced the texting function with each other, alternately swearing and giggling. "Right, Missus. But what about Mr. Neil?"

"He'll probably stay till dawn. He can hail a camel."

Neil took her arm as she emerged, smiling for the photographers.

"One more thing," he muttered as they were ushered through immense wooden doors. "Do not mention God."

They joined the crowd packed in the enormous foyer, waiting their turn to go through the receiving line. Celeste thought she hadn't seen one this long since her brother's bar mitzvah in 1962. Celeste had grown up in small-town Texas, where there were few Jews. There were a lot of jokes like "Ride 'em, Jewboy," but those were good-natured. Mostly.

Stretching her neck, she tried to catch sight of Abby and Elaine. It would make more sense to look for their husbands, since Ted and Richard—and Neil, for that matter—were all taller than most British men, but she saw only a sea of haute couture, sequins glittering under monstrous chandeliers. It was like being backstage at New York Fashion Week.

Servants, all men, dressed in vaguely military white uniforms, moved through the crowd taking coats and giving guests a numbered ticket. Celeste reluctantly shrugged off her leather motorcycle jacket and handed it over. Biker jackets over evening gowns were a new thing, and she loved the look: the tough leather seemed to rebuke the flimsy opulence of the gowns, a reminder of the world that lay outside grand houses like this. But without the jacket she was just a fiftyish woman in a plain blue Valentino, though it *was* embroidered with silver thread that *did* complement the silver strands in her hair.

Celeste examined the numbered ticket she'd been given. It looked more like a wedding invitation: all script and raised gold letters.

"Wow," she said. "If the coat tickets are this fancy, imagine the toilet paper."

Neil pinched her arm, dropping his hand before she could smack it. This was an old game between them. "Behave," he muttered. "You promised."

Instead of pinching back, Celeste sneezed. Neil flinched. She knew that look.

"I'm not sick," she assured him. "Therefore, you will not get sick. It's that perfume."

Heavy perfume, unlike real flowers, always made Celeste sneeze. She recognized this one—she'd been ambushed by scent girls with atomizers at Harrods often enough. It was new, expensive, and complex, enveloping the guests like a chemical cloud. *Strategy*, that's what it was called. Too rich for her taste, in every sense of the word. She wondered whether it was the sheik wearing it or one of his wives.

Cold air flowed into the house from the open doors. Celeste shivered, wishing for her jacket, as she took in the marble floor, twenty-foot ceiling, and massive staircase gleaming with gold trim. The line shuffled forward. Eventually she could see into a massive ballroom painted the exact shade of blue you'd expect to see in Heaven, with pointed arched doorways leading to the rest of the house. Celeste could not see what lay beyond. Music playing over a superior sound system seemed stirring, regal, familiar. Handel's *Water Music*, written for an English king.

"Are we meeting George the First?" she murmured to Neil, who pinched her arm again.

Finally, another servant led them toward a platform where four people waited on velvet-and-gilt chairs that resembled thrones.

The man in the first chair rose to greet them. He was not tall but solid, barrel-chested, as if a hug from him could crack your ribs, though he didn't look like someone who did much hugging.

He wore glasses, a goatee, and immaculate flowing white robes with a traditional headdress, made of such fine cloth and constructed so well that Celeste suspected they, too, were haute couture. Was Armani doing Arab robes now?

"Peace be upon you, Neil Stoneman," said the sheik, extending his hand without hesitation. "It is good to see you again. We have much to discuss."

"Indeed, we do, sir," said Neil, shaking hands. He tugged Celeste forward. "Sheik Muhktar Farouqi, this is my...this is Celeste Stoneman."

The sheik did not offer his hand but inclined his head. "I am most honored, madam. Welcome to *Bayt Hadiqua*: House of Gardens."

"Thank you for inviting us," said Celeste. "Everything is so... impressive."

The sheik smiled. "Yes." He held out an arm to the handsome young man beside him, who also rose to shake hands. "My son, Tariq." He did not bother to disguise the pride in his voice.

Tariq was no taller than the sheik, but, oddly, his head looked as if it belonged to a bigger man—as though Nature had played some kind of trick. It looked *wrong*. Unlike his father, Tariq reached for Celeste's hand. For a moment she thought he was going to kiss it.

"A true pleasure," he said. His eyes, dark and brilliant, looked as if they'd been outlined in kohl. Celeste permitted herself the sexist thought that eyes like that were wasted on a man. He was elegant in his hand-tailored tuxedo, though he probably looked just as perfect in jeans. With apparent reluctance he let her withdraw her fingers, holding on a moment too long, no doubt a practiced move. This was a man who thought he knew women. A player for sure.

Turning to the seated women, he said: "May I introduce my mother, Begum, and my father's second wife, Mehraj?"

Celeste managed not to sneeze at the renewed blast of *Strategy.* The women placed a hand over their hearts in greeting but said nothing.

"How do you do, Mrs. Farouqi?" said Celeste, then realized she'd have to call the younger woman the same thing.

But Neil hissed in her ear: "Say *Madam*," and she corrected herself.

Begum, who looked older than her husband, sat very upright in her purple satin gown with its tiered capelet, just the thing to skim over bulges and conceal fleshy arms. Mehraj, much younger and smiling, wore body-hugging gold lamé with tiny straps and an open back. With effort, Celeste kept her face blank, realizing that some part of her had been expecting harem pants and ankle bells. Both women wore pounds of jewelry, and Mehraj had pasted gold sequins to her eyelids.

As they moved on, Celeste whispered in Neil's ear: "Don't you think Begum looks like Golda Meir?"

He stiffened. "Please don't repeat that to anyone."

Now she pinched his arm. "Relax. I just like to torture you."

"I remember. Vividly."

"Well, you deserved it. You dumped me for a younger woman. Good thing I like her. Good thing I like skipping all those boring business dinners."

"I need a drink."

"Will there be any booze? Or just milk and cookies?"

Neil laughed. "Oh no, the champagne will flow. One of the reasons Jadalis visit the West is so they can openly indulge."

As if to prove his point, a young man—all the servers were men—in a white shirt and bow tie stopped to offer a tray of flutes filled with champagne, while another proffered a tray of hors d'oeuvres.

"Care for a *samboosak*?" he asked. Working-class British accent—a caterer, probably, unlike the stern security guards, who all looked Jadali.

Careful to use their right hands—even Neil, who was a lefty— they bit into savory lamb pastries and moved off to mingle with the other guests.

"There they are!" Neil exclaimed in obvious relief. He'd spotted Ted and Richard, so that meant Abby and Elaine were nearby. Neil steered her through the crowd toward their friends.

The men immediately went into a huddle while the women noted each other's gowns. Elaine was wearing her silk palazzo pants and beaded jacket, Abby her red Dior. They'd all seen each other's outfits before but exclaimed over them anyway—it was as much a ritual as the sheik's formal nod. Now if Willow had come, she'd have worn something startling, like a glittery tangerine bra top with matching bicycle shorts. Willow liked to shock. But she was off spreading make-up gospel, and everyone else looked conventional enough.

They sipped champagne and studied the crowd. It was an international mix, though you could always pick out the Americans because they laughed so loud and touched so much—arms, shoulders, backs.

"Some shindig," Celeste commented. "Look at all the shiny."

"I hear Princess Di was invited but had to decline," said Elaine. "Not an official function."

"Aren't the Farouqis royalty themselves?" asked Abby.

"No, but they're all in bed together. Neil says the Jadali princes get a cut of every cent the sheik makes, which is why the sheik gets all the juicy contracts."

"I hope we get a tour of the house," said Abby, glancing around the enormous ballroom.

"We won't," said Elaine. "Did you see all that security?"

"Oh, speaking of security," said Celeste. "I took Willow to the airport this morning, and—"

Elaine interrupted with a scowl: "Why do you insist on befriending your ex-husband's trophy wife? Do you really think that's healthy?"

"But I *like* Willow. And I *love* Max. And you know very well that Neil didn't even meet her till after the divorce." She shrugged. "He wanted a child."

"A *blood* child," Elaine said darkly. "You could have adopted."

"Lainey." Celeste squeezed her shoulder. "You've got to get over this. If *I* can let it go, why can't you?"

"Because you're my closest friend and I hate to see you

cheated."

Elaine had a son and Abby had twin daughters, all tucked safely away at Ivies in the States. It was true that Celeste had always yearned for a child, but she'd made her peace with it, she had a good life, and she'd worked hard on herself to get here.

"Listen," she said without heat. "Everybody's okay, so don't worry."

"*Someone* should worry about you," Elaine muttered. "I think you're in denial."

"I think *you* should try Prozac. You're the one who's depressed."

"Me?" Elaine looked offended. "I'm not depressed. I'm just a bitch."

They all laughed, raising their glasses. No one disagreed.

"*Any*way," said Abby, always the peacemaker. "You were saying, Celeste? The airport? Security?"

"When we got there, Willow's plane was ready, but the security guards made us wait behind the barrier while another jet unloaded passengers. It was pouring, the wind was brutal, and Willow and I were sharing my umbrella. But we all had to stand and wait while they rolled the stairway up and passengers began getting off. I thought it had to be royalty, or at least rock stars, but all I saw was a cloud of billowing white robes. Then one of the security guards poked the other and squealed like a little girl: 'Ooh, *super,* Clive! More bloody ragheads! Maybe *this* lot's here to buy Big Ben!' Willow wasn't allowed to board her plane until every last one of them disappeared into limousines."

"VIPs?" asked Abby. "Diplomats, maybe?"

Celeste shrugged. "It was a private plane."

They all turned to look at the robed sheik as he flowed through the crowd, pausing to chat with guests.

"Related to him, you think?" Abby asked. When Elaine snorted, she protested: "What? Don't they all marry their cousins?"

"Abby," said Celeste. "Don't be a bigot."

"I'm not!"

"No more bigoted than Brits are against Americans," Elaine said dryly. "Or Americans against Brits."

This was not a safe topic for a crowded room, so Celeste asked: "Where are the boys?"

"Off moving vast sums of money," said Elaine.

"What about us? What should we do tomorrow?" asked Abby.

"We could try the new step class," Celeste said without enthusiasm. "Or that Boxercise thing. Or that therapy where they put crystals between your toes."

"There's a meeting of Britons for Bosnia," said Abby, also without enthusiasm.

"I refuse to sit through another endless afternoon of women speaking without moving their jaws," Elaine snapped. "It was one thing when we were actually collecting food and clothing —I mean, we were *doing* something. Now we only seem to *talk*. In fact—" she turned a defiant eye on her friends—"I'm sick of meetings, period. So many good causes, yes: breast cancer, prison reform, literacy—I *care* about them, but I'm just not interested in *hearing* any more about them. Is that a terrible thing to say?"

"You're saying what the rest of us feel." Celeste patted Elaine's arm.

"We could go get new highlights," Abby said doubtfully.

"That takes forever," said Celeste. "I hate sitting in that chair."

Abby gave up. "Oh, let's just go antique-shopping."

"We always go antique-shopping," said Celeste. "And I don't even *have* antiques."

Unlike Abby and Elaine, who loved to scavenge for treasures on Portobello Road, Celeste had decorated her post-divorce home in clean simple lines. She was proud of owning the only modern house in her expat neighborhood. She'd hated the traditional marble-clad townhouses everyone else seemed to go for—they were narrow and dark and cluttered with breakables. Celeste was from Texas: she needed air and space and light. This house suited her, and the generous back yard and garage apartment for domestic help had sealed the deal.

"Well then," Abby was saying. "What are we going to *do*?"

"I hear vaginal steaming is a thing," Celeste said brightly. "Apparently, they do it with mugwort and wormwood. After that, we could go get our eyebrows tattooed."

Abby looked horrified. Elaine shuddered.

"And then go to lunch," Celeste finished. "We'll go to lunch three or four times. That should fill up the day."

"Oh, not the place with the éclairs!" said Abby. "Not unless we do aerobics first!"

"Ladies," someone said behind them. The voice was rich and amused. Tariq, the sheik's son. Celeste wondered how much he had heard. "I hope you are enjoying yourselves."

Tariq had the ability to hold your gaze so intently, with such perfect stillness, that Celeste thought it was most certainly a practiced effect. She took a step back. She didn't know why—it was instinctive.

"Your new house is lovely," Abby said shyly.

Tariq smiled, his teeth ridiculously white. "*Hadiqa* means *garden*. Did you know it is built over an underground river? In The Judgments, Paradise is described as a magnificent garden growing over such a river. My father was very pleased."

Apparently, the sheik didn't know that the sunken river beneath his new mansion was actually a sewer and had been for centuries.

"The gardens are barren now," Tariq continued, "but you must come back in Spring to see them bloom." Then, to her surprise, he turned to Celeste. "And Neil says you enjoy art, Mrs. Stoneman?"

"Some kinds."

"Well then, you must have a look at the pieces my father has chosen. There are antique tile mosaics, quite magnificent. And a number of antiquities on display. Plus, his beloved horse sculptures."

But before she could respond, they were interrupted by a voice over the sound system.

"Ladies and gentlemen," it said. "Sheik Muhktar Farouqi and

his family welcome you to *Hadiqa House* and hope you will enjoy this performance of the Sword Circle, traditional Jadali music and dance."

The Handel stopped, replaced by drums, reed flutes, some kind of stringed instrument, and a chorus of nasal male voices, twining and looping in the long plaintive tones that reminded Celeste of a cantor chanting *Kol Nidre*, the yearly plea for forgiveness. And that made her wonder yet again how different Arabs and Jews really could be: after all, Isaac and Ishmael were both sons of Abraham. All their descendants were cousins, were they not?

Meanwhile, the platform and thrones had been whisked away. From one of the arched doorways, a line of men dressed in black robes and white headdresses emerged, bobbing to the rhythm, each whirling a sword above his head. The hilts were adorned with thick golden tassels that bounced as the men formed a circle. First, they moved as a group, raising and lowering the swords, keeping the rhythm. Then, two at a time, they met in the middle of the circle for a mock sword fight; each pair fought/ danced in perfect symmetry, leaping and dodging with one-footed hops. It was practiced and graceful, still a *dance* though it evoked battle. It reminded Celeste of the feverish circle-dances at her Orthodox cousin's wedding.

The guests were motionless, rapt. The sheik might not know that this in itself was a great compliment: Celeste had been to many formal events where the guests kept chattering through a violinist's or soprano's performance. Then again, these dancers did have *swords*.

When the men finally exited, still bobbing to the beat, the guests applauded and the music faded, replaced immediately by soft familiar jazz. But it was not coming through the sound system. Everyone watched as the uniformed servants deftly whisked away a screen of greenery, revealing a twelve-piece orchestra conducted by a bald, wizened runt of an old man, vigorously waving his baton.

"Good Lord," said Elaine. "Is that Lester Lanin?"

Celeste would have to remind her not to mention God.

"He must be eighty!" Abby exclaimed.

"At least! He's been playing since the stock market crash," said Elaine. "He's played for the White House. For the Queen."

Lester Lanin was known for taking his cues by watching people dance to his music. Was dancing permissible? Probably not in Jadal—unless men danced with men and women with women, like at her cousin's wedding—but what about here? She hid a smile, wondering if the sheik knew that little old Lester Lanin was a Jew.

When the waiters reappeared, everyone took a fresh drink, including Tariq. "Did you enjoy the sword dance, ladies?" he asked.

"Very much," said Celeste.

"Can you do it too?" Abby asked.

He grinned. "Not only can I do it, I can spin in the middle with a lit candelabra on my head."

Celeste decided not to mention the old men at her cousin's wedding whirling in the circle with full bottles of wine on their heads.

"Jadali dances are based on our nomad roots," said Tariq. "At one time we were *all* Bedu, so we try to preserve the culture, the blood." He turned his grin on Abby. "And that, madam, is why we tend to marry our cousins."

Abby clapped her hand over her mouth with a muffled squeak.

"Your English is flawless, Mr. Farouqi," Celeste said to divert his attention.

He bowed in thanks. "Perhaps because I am always using it. I have my own flat in the city. I live here most of the year to look after my father's business interests. And my own," he added.

Celeste was tempted to ask if he drove a red Lamborghini, but that was impertinent, and she'd promised to behave herself. Before she could say anything else, the husbands popped up along with the sheik himself. Celeste took a closer look at his pristine white robes. Neil had warned her not to touch his headdress—it was considered a great insult—which of course made her perverse little fingers itch to reach out and flick it. Though there were other guests from the Middle East, the sheik was the only one in traditional robes. Celeste thought he probably *wanted* to emphasize his difference, his success, here in infidel territory. So unlike the British, who would rather swallow nails than be caught boasting, though they were masters of the understated and obliterating put-down.

Muhktar wanted to know if his American friends were enjoying themselves, if they'd liked the Sword Circle, if there was anything he could do to increase their pleasure. When he had asked and been answered three times, he dropped his voice, turning to the husbands: "I understand you gentlemen are great fans of British football. I am considering buying into a club, but I'm not sure which one. Perhaps you could advise me?"

Ted, Neil, and Richard lit up like Christmas morning and started naming teams—Arsenal, Liverpool, Manchester United —then arguing about goal averages. As the sheik glided on, they followed, voices raised, wives trailing.

Celeste looked back at Tariq and read his grin correctly. "He's flattering them, isn't he?"

"Well," Tariq replied. "If he really wanted advice about buying an English soccer club, he'd ask the English, don't you think?"

He didn't wait for an answer, merely raised his glass of champagne, and slipped away. Celeste, unclaimed, began drifting around the ballroom, feeling like the spinster heroine in a Jane Austen novel, a sensation she rather enjoyed.

Muhktar Farouqi interested her. His smile was polite, and he touched no one; he glided through the crowd, perfectly contained. What was it like to contain so much power? All that money, all that influence, the ability to *change* things—surely that was the essence of power. He seemed utterly solid and opaque, revealing nothing of what was going on behind those dark eyes, nowhere near as beautiful as his son's. What would it be like to be married to such a man? In Jadal, all men ruled their wives. Who did their wives rule?

Celeste caught sight of the younger wife, Mehraj, in her sparkling gown, jewels flashing at ears and throat. Instead of mingling like her husband, she was stationed off to the side, surrounded by women. Was that accidental or by design? Celeste couldn't see Begum at all.

Couples had begun tentatively box-stepping to Lester Lanin's jazzy pop standards. The sheik looked on benevolently as if watching children in a sandbox. Glad that she didn't have to dance, with or without a sword, Celeste threaded her way around the perimeter, wondering what lay beyond the pointed archways. She stopped and peered down one corridor. Guests were probably not supposed to wander off by themselves, but Tariq *had* told her to be sure to look at the art. And she could see even from the threshold that there were pictures hung on the wall and glass cases with objects inside. Surely she could venture just a few steps in.

The pictures, she soon realized, weren't paintings but the mosaics Tariq had mentioned: panels of jewel-like tiles, brilliantly restored interlocking designs of geometrical shapes, flowers and vines, eight-pointed stars, flowing Arabic script. The renewed colors looked so fresh they seemed to shimmer: gold, tomato-red, cobalt, green, black. Each tile stood alone, a self-contained whole, but each also helped complete the overall design.

Lit glass cases displayed the antiquities: goblets patterned with similar designs, elegant coffee urns, bottles and bowls glazed with metallic luster. How ancient were they? When had they been discovered? They looked as if they belonged in a museum. If these objects were genuine, they must be priceless— the rumors of the Farouqis' obscene wealth must be true.

She kept wandering, turning corners, peeking into rooms, admiring the hand-woven carpets, wondering if she could sneak upstairs to look around. But as she lingered in an alcove to admire an enormous hookah of silver and glass with tubes dangling like snakes, she heard a baby wail.

Though Celeste had never, would never, have a child of her

own, whenever she heard a baby, she alerted like a doe raising its head. It was an instinct, as if someone had called her name. When children in the park cried "Mummy," she turned around, though no one had ever addressed her that way. And when she heard a baby cry, her heart sped up, her nipples briefly ached. No doubt she was a couch case, but she could not stop herself from following the baby's wail. Then she heard the slap.

It was definitely a slap. There was no mistaking the sound of a human hand smacking human flesh. *Was someone hurting the baby?*

She located the room the cries were coming from, stopping just outside the door to stifle a sneeze. A cloud of *Strategy* hung in the air like a dark presence. Within, Begum, the sheik's first wife, was thrusting a wailing baby into the arms of a very thin, very young woman—a servant, to judge by the long plain dress and hair-concealing scarf. Really, she wasn't much more than a girl, maybe a teenager. The girl clutched the baby and hurried out of the room. Celeste stepped back out of sight. But Begum was still scolding. And slapping. And maybe worse, from the thuds and grunts Celeste could hear. She peered into the room again.

Begum was indeed beating someone. "*Khara!*" she kept saying, as she bent over another thin young girl. "*Sharmoota!*"

"*La!*" cried the girl, trying to ward off the blows. "*La! La! Kafa ean! Tawaquf ean dhlk!*"

You didn't have to speak Arabic to know that the older woman was calling the younger nasty names, and the younger was pleading with her to stop. *That* language was universal.

Now Begum used her fists to punch the girl, who doubled up, knees to chest, protecting her belly rather than her head. Celeste sent a wild look up and down the corridor. Who could she call to help?

Begum drew back her foot to kick the girl in the stomach. Celeste sucked in her breath to scream, but the girl beat her to it. The scream was surprisingly powerful.

"*Akhrs!*" Begum hissed, dropping her foot. "*Akhrs!*" She gave the girl a final slap, then smoothed her purple gown and turned toward the door. Celeste hastily withdrew. Begum lumbered out, turning toward the kitchen, where the caterers were noisily at work. When she was gone, Celeste rushed into the room and bent over the weeping girl.

"Are you all right?" she said, knowing the girl probably couldn't understand but helpless not to ask. "Where are you hurt?"

She helped the girl turn over, then gasped. This girl was just as thin as the other—gaunt face, spindly arms and legs—but her belly was swollen. And that's where Begum had been concentrating her blows. She'd been about to kick a pregnant girl in the belly.

The girl's sobs were subsiding, but she would not look Celeste in the eye. Celeste gently tipped up her chin and brushed the backs of her fingers over the girl's wet face, prompting a look of surprise, even shock. This girl was not used to a tender touch.

Celeste made up her mind. Whatever the consequences, she would deal with them tomorrow. What mattered right now was saving this child, getting her away from this house of horrors. *Hadiqa House*, indeed! Celeste used the hem of her Valentino to wipe the girl's face and looked her in the eye. "Listen. We're going to get you out of here, all right?"

Of course, the girl didn't understand the English words, but Celeste hoped the intention was clear from her tone, that this too was a universal language.

"Celeste," she said, patting her own chest.

Hiccupping, the girl copied her. "Najima."

Celeste held out her arms and mimicked pushing up sleeves. The girl hesitated, then bared her own arms. As Celeste had suspected, they were covered with scars and bruises, old, new, and in between. This beating was not a solitary incident. Celeste gestured toward Najima's legs and looked a question. Najima nodded, then circled her hand above her torso. Everywhere. She had been beaten all over her body. And Begum had definitely been focusing on that swollen belly. Briefly Celeste wondered who the father was, but no time to think about that now. She had to figure out what to do. Or rather, how to do it. She already knew what.

Helping Najima stand, Celeste dug her new phone out of her evening bag, praying that Benny was indeed standing by. She was going to have to text him—she couldn't risk being overheard—but if he'd stopped for a pint at the pub, he might not hear the *ping*.

Laboriously, she typed in the message: *Come NOW drive around back to service entrance NO LIGHTS come FAST!*

Then, one arm around Najima, Celeste ventured into the corridor. It barely registered that no one had come to investigate the girl's scream. Perhaps screams were not uncommon in this household. She could hear banging and thumping and raised voices in the kitchen and steered Najima toward the noise, stopping just outside the doorway. There had to be a service entrance. She risked a glance within. Begum was gone and the kitchen was seething, but it was controlled chaos, all the catering staff engaged in some frenzied activity. These must be the cooks: unlike the servers with their crisp shirts and bow ties, they were dressed in standard kitchen whites. Bags of trash were piled near a sturdy door, standing ajar to let the cool air in, along with a heap of dirty laundry: towels, cloth napkins, stained uniforms. That gave Celeste her *how*.

Pushing Najima gently against the wall, indicating she should stay put, Celeste slipped into the kitchen. No one seemed to notice. On a table she saw a bowl with the oily remains of a bean dip. Inspired, she scooped up a handful and smeared it down the front of her dress—ruining it, of course, but she was tired of Valentino anyway. Then she approached a worker who was washing platters in the sink, his paper head-cover, which looked like a shower cap, drooping from his back pocket. Celeste plucked it out at the same moment she tapped his shoulder. It seemed she was a natural pickpocket: the young man only looked up, saying politely: "Yes madam, how may I help you?"

Celeste gave him a rueful grin and indicated the huge stain on her dress. "Could I possibly have a clean wet rag? I'll try to repair the damage."

"Of course." He let the water run cold, soaked a clean dishcloth, and wrung it out. "Shall I...?" he asked uneasily. The stain was directly over her bosom.

"No thanks, I'll do it." She took the wet cloth. "Let me just get out of everyone's way."

He nodded in relief and went back to his platters. Dabbing at the stain, Celeste drifted toward the service door and the heap of soiled linens. When no one was watching, she snatched up a white double-breasted jacket and a pair of pants, both smeared with red—tomato sauce, she hoped—and swiftly exited the kitchen, depending on her Primary Principle: if you act as if you know what you're doing, people tend to leave you alone. Sure enough, no one seemed to notice.

Najima was still leaning against the wall. She made no protest as Celeste thrust her arms into the jacket and buttoned it all the way, then helped her step into the pants, stuffing her long skirt down the front and rolling up the cuffs so the girl wouldn't trip. But when Celeste tugged at her headscarf—that had to go; it was a dead giveaway—Najima resisted, trying to hold it in place. Celeste showed her the paper cap she'd lifted. She pointed at the kitchen in what she hoped was still universal language: *This is how we get you out of here.* Najima, not slow to understand, dropped her hands, and let Celeste tug off the headscarf. For a moment Celeste just stared. The girl's hair had been brutally hacked off. It looked like a three-year-old had done the job: ragged tufts standing up in some places, scalp showing in others. Someone had done this to her in anger. With a knife, apparently.

Then she heard the little *ping* from her phone. Glancing down, she saw Benny's message: *Outside by catering vans.*

"Come on." Celeste covered Najima's pitiful scalp with the paper hat, took her arm, and, with a reassuring squeeze, again put her Primary Principle into action. They moved across the kitchen. They reached the door. They went through the door.

The big white catering vans were parked in the service area and on the other side, long and dark, no headlights burning, the discreetly rumbling limo. God bless Benny.

He started to get out, but Celeste said: "No, just go," tumbling Najima and herself onto the back seat. As they coasted down the long drive toward the gate, Celeste gently pushed Najima onto the floor, looking for her leather jacket until she remembered that, of course, it was still in the house. Instead, she draped the hem of her ruined Valentino—which really had turned out to be worth its price—over the shaking girl's head and scattered Benny's newspaper over the rest of her. The car rolled past the security guards, Celeste serenely turning her hand from side to side, waving like the Queen.

When they were clear, she helped Najima climb back onto the seat and told Benny to turn up the heat.

"Where to, Missus?" Benny asked. That was what he always called her. Flora too—apparently that particular class barrier could not be jumped in Britain.

Flora! That was the answer! Celeste had been debating between police, hospital, or embassy, but Flora had grown up in the Middle East and she spoke Arabic.

"Home, Benny," she replied. "Take us home."

CHAPTER TWO

lora fingered the tiny gold cross around her neck. Her mother had given her that cross when it was finally safe to wear—the day they left the Middle East. They'd already left the Philippines when she was small for lucrative work in the Jadali construction industry. Flora had grown up there, attending an international school where she learned both Arabic and English. Her father, though independently employed, spoke grimly of the *Kafala* system—allegedly a foreign worker sponsorship program, although in practice more like slavery: workers were not given adequate wages or time off; their visas were confiscated; they could not leave without their employer's permission. Flora and her mother had followed her father from site to site, living as frugally as possible, until the family saved enough money to bribe their way to England, hoping for a better life.

When Mrs. Celeste rang from the car, explaining briefly what she'd done, Flora assumed the girl was either *Kafala* or worse: some poor families still sold their own children into servitude. And impoverished pilgrims from other lands making the Haj sometimes sold their daughters so they could afford the trip home. Girls in the *souk* could be snatched for prostitution or organ-harvesting when their mothers weren't looking. Flora had heard the horror stories. She knew this girl had been through hell.

But she hadn't expected her to be so young. Or pregnant. The poor starved creature was still a child herself. And what had been done to her hair? Flora and the girl looked at each other, their faces the same warm speckled brown as Flora's famous gingersnaps. Then Flora unfolded the fluffy blanket she'd brought downstairs, held it out, and the girl stepped forward into her embrace.

"*Ahlan wa sahlan, binti,*" Flora said. "Welcome, daughter."

The girl burst into tears.

Flora rocked her a bit, murmuring: "*Alhamdulillah as-salameh.* Thank God you are here safely."

The girl mumbled the ritual response: "*Allah ya selmek.*" May God protect you.

Then Celeste said briskly: "I think a warm bath first, don't you? We need to check her injuries. And then food."

Flora nodded. "There's vegetable soup in the fridge. And I baked today."

Celeste smiled. "She needs whole milk too. Benny, would you run out and get some?"

"Right, Missus!" He was gone almost before she finished speaking.

While Flora took Najima upstairs for her bath, Celeste headed into the kitchen to heat soup and leave messages on Abby's and Elaine's answering machines. Forget tattooed eyebrows and vaginal steaming: this was a true emergency. They had to meet tomorrow and figure out what to do next.

Flora brought a warm flannel nightgown from Celeste's drawer into the bathroom where Najima soaked in the big tub, still looking stunned. Before Flora turned on the taps and urged her inside, the girl had taken the thick washcloth and jasmine soap Flora offered and started scrubbing the tub. She thought she was meant to clean the bathroom. Flora set her straight and helped her in, discreetly inspecting her wounds. Bruises and scars in various stages of healing, but no broken bones at the moment. Like all pregnant women, Najima kept one hand laid over her belly. When she realized that Flora did not expect her to get out of the tub immediately, her shoulders relaxed. Flora ran more hot water. Finally, she said in Arabic: "Who is the father?"

The girl froze, looking down.

"It is not your shame," Flora said firmly. "It is his. Tell me your story, daughter." When the girl remained silent, she added: "You are safe now. We are friends. We will not send you back to those monsters."

At the word *wahush*—monsters—the girl looked up, startled. Flora thought she was most likely still in shock: grieving would come later. After a moment, Najima began to speak, her eyes fixed on Flora's gold cross. She described the slave-trader's visit, Ghassan's warning about family honor, the mansion in Jadal where she was taught how to use a vacuum cleaner and washing machine, then made to work eighteen-hour days and never allowed outside. If the children cried, the maids were punished.

"Once," she said, agitated enough to look Flora in the eye, "Madame Mehraj's baby was teething and wouldn't stop crying. Jameelah was scared Madame Begum would beat us again, so I told her to go pick some poppies in the garden, which I could scrape for the thick white gum that soothes pain. That's what my mother always did. But Jameelah was caught outside and whipped, and—" her gaze dropped again—"it was my fault."

Flora tipped up the girl's chin. "No, it was not, and I think you know that. If a *shaytun* chooses to torment a victim, is it the victim's fault?"

Tears filled Najima's eyes. "They're still there," she whispered. "Jameelah. Dafiyah. Fadeelah. The *Amreekiyah* rescued me, but they're still there and Madame will punish them for what I've done."

Flora studied her. Three more girls—slaves—being abused and molested. Would the authorities help? Would they dare oppose a man as rich and powerful as the sheik? Flora knew they wouldn't listen to her. But Mrs. Celeste was smart. And despite being a spoiled rich lady, she was kind. She would know what to do.

Flora plucked the enormous towel from the heater. "Bath-time is over," she said. "Let's go downstairs, get you some food, and talk to the *Amreekiyah*."

After Najima finished her second bowl of soup, her third glass of milk, and her fourth gingersnap, Flora said: "Tell Mrs. Celeste what happened to you. I will translate, but I want her to hear it in your own voice." She stood behind Najima, hands on her shoulders. "Go on, *habibti*. Tell us."

The endearment made Najima flinch—it had been a long time since anyone had called her "dear one."

"Two years ago, when I was thirteen, the slave-trader came," she began, and told them the rest of the story. "In the mansion, the girls and I did all the cleaning. Madame Begum would stand over us as we washed dishes, making us rinse them without letting them touch the sink. If they touched the sink, we had to start over. We had to scrub the floor tile by tile until it was *puk*—religiously clean. We took care of the children, but if they cried or misbehaved, we were punished. We were not permitted to discipline the children ourselves, so we tried very hard to keep them happy, keep them quiet. We were not permitted to use the furniture, not even to sit on a chair when feeding the children. We were fed fruit peels and whatever the family left on their plates after eating. To punish us, they would throw this leftover food out. And beat us. And other things."

She stopped.

Flora laid a hand on the girl's mutilated head. Najima's eyes closed. The last person to touch her like this was Zainab, her mother.

"Who did that to your hair?" Celeste asked through Flora.

"Madame Begum. It was a punishment—she said she got ill because I looked at her food."

Benny uttered a nasty word, then instantly apologized. He rubbed his round face, lurched up to peer out the window, sat back down. Celeste had never seen him so agitated—she'd nicknamed him Buddha because he was so tubby and cheerful and calm.

"So, they brought you to England," she said, prompting Najima. Flora resumed translating.

"I don't remember much about the trip. I had never seen an airplane before. They gave us something to drink that made us sleep. Whenever we woke, we had to drink more. We were very sick from the drink, but we had to start working right away when we reached the new house." She leaned forward and spoke urgently. "There are three more girls like me. All the other servants are men, even the cook. But they chose to work for the family, and they have passports: they can leave."

"A passport," Celeste said. "Doesn't she have one too? How could she enter the country without it?"

"Bribes," said Flora. "The sheik probably bought fake papers. And even if they were real, he'd have confiscated them so the girls couldn't leave. Not that they'd have anywhere to go."

"Do the men bother you?" Celeste asked softly.

Najima looked down. "They have strict orders not to...violate us. But that doesn't stop them from handling us. They touch us anywhere they want, however they want. They help themselves to our bodies."

"Who is the father of your baby?" It was a question all of them were burning to know.

Najima did not answer at first. Flora murmured in her ear. Finally, the girl whispered: "The master. The sheik. He caught me in the laundry room. We girls—we try never to be alone. But he caught me."

Celeste was dumbfounded. She'd been certain it was Tariq. But that powerful man, old enough to be Najima's grandfather, a man with two wives, for God's sake! She wanted to march back over and slap his smug face. More than that: beat him bloody with a good American baseball bat. She gulped her cold tea, trying to bring her temper under control. Tantrums would not help Najima, nor the other girls still trapped in the house.

"Mrs. Celeste," said Flora. "This situation is more serious than you know. The sheik's son will not want this baby to be born."

"Why not? What does he care?"

"He is the only son, yes? That means he is the only heir to that great fortune—girls do not inherit. But according to The Judgments, any male child—even the son of a slave—must share equally in the inheritance." Flora slowly shook her head. "Believe me, he does not want any brothers. He does not sound like a man who likes to share."

"What are you saying?"

"Tariq will surely try to kill Najima. He would have done so anyway, but now that she's missing, he will be frantic to find her and destroy the child."

Benny exploded. "Let him bloody well try! He'll have to go through me first!"

"Through all of us," said Celeste. "But a man like that, with unlimited resources…"

Najima, who had not been following the English part of the conversation, suddenly broke in, her voice urgent.

"She is begging you to rescue the other girls," Flora said. "She says Madame Begum will punish them for her escape."

"And that's on me," said Celeste. "She didn't ask to be rescued —I decided for her. So, I have to fix it. Tell her we will find a way."

When Flora translated, Najima slid off the chair onto her knees. She clasped her hands, saying over and over, her voice breaking: "*Shukran, shukran.*"

"She's thanking you," Flora said.

"So I gathered. How do you say, 'Don't thank me for righting this terrible wrong'?"

"*La shukran ala wajib*, more or less."

Slowly Celeste repeated the words as tears spilled down Najima's cheeks. She tried to press her forehead to Celeste's feet, but no one let her.

"You are a free person now," Flora told her. "You will never be anyone's slave again."

"But where will I go? What will I do?"

"We have lots of time to figure that out. Meanwhile, you need a good night's sleep."

Najima couldn't help leaning against Flora. The flannel nightgown and fleece robe—the most exotic garments Najima had ever seen—embraced her body in luxurious warmth. Of course, she had no winter clothing of her own. Nor—

She turned her face into Flora's shoulder and mumbled something.

"She says she is ashamed because she does not have clean underwear for tomorrow," Flora said.

Celeste's eyes filled. She was pretty sure Benny's did too.

"We'll buy whatever you need tomorrow," she said, then looked at Flora. "And maybe your midwife friend—"

"Myrtle," Flora supplied.

"Yes, Myrtle. Maybe she could come by and take a look? Tell us what Najima needs—vitamins and so forth? I think it's best to keep her out of public view."

Flora patted Najima's head. "And we'll see what we can do about that hair."

"And I'll go to the shops and fetch everything she needs," Benny declared.

Celeste smiled at him. "You'll go buy women's underwear, Benny?"

He looked affronted. "And why not?"

Flora and Celeste exchanged an amused glance. "Why not indeed?" Celeste said. "We need more like you, Benny." She turned to Najima. "Now off to bed—you need a good long sleep. We'll talk more tomorrow."

Flora took Najima's arm and guided her to the stairs. *Shukrans* floated back over her shoulder until the girl was out of sight.

Celeste booted up the Answer Box and started a pot of coffee. She too needed a good long sleep, but she knew she wasn't getting one tonight.

Najima woke in a panic: the sun was fully up, she was late,

she would be beaten for sure...then she saw the magnificent room and remembered. For once she had not dreamed of being chased by white war horses thundering across the desert. In fact, she hadn't slept so deeply since she was sold—the bed felt as if it were indeed stuffed with the fabled ostrich feathers. She saw a neatly folded pile of clothing on the chair—what slave had a chair in her bedroom? what slave had a room to herself, with her own bathroom? —and got up to investigate. Clean underwear, drawstring pants, a loose top. They must belong to the *Amreekiyah*. Mrs. Celeste. Najima's own dirty clothes were nowhere in sight. Hesitant—imagine Madam Begum or Mehraj ever offering a maid their own personal garments: they would sooner burn them!—she put on the new things, marveling at the soft cloth on her skin.

The bathroom was as grand as any in the Farouqi household, certainly finer than the facilities designated for the maids. She was reluctant to use the plush washcloth and towel laid out for her, but they were the only ones she saw. She washed herself, used the new toothbrush, then confronted the toilet. She was still getting used to English toilets. According to The Judgments, a person's bottom was forbidden to have any contact with urine. Gingerly, she lifted the seat and squatted over the toilet as if it were the familiar hole in the floor.

After wiping down the bathroom, she made the bed, checked the carpet for lint, and, finding nothing else to tidy, stared out the window at the low clouded skies. This feeble English sun was nothing like the glaring light of Jadal. Then she told herself she had stalled long enough. It was time to go downstairs.

Mrs. Celeste's house was like none she had seen: the furniture was simple and solid, made of blond wood, with bright pictures crowding the walls. So many pictures of big, beautiful flowers. Perhaps this was Mrs. Celeste's garden. Perhaps the house was full of light to make up for the bleakness outside—perhaps the place Mrs. Celeste came from was full of light, and she missed it. At any rate, this house felt happy. Najima would ask Mrs. Flora to tell Mrs. Celeste how eager she was to perform each and every task assigned her. She would work harder than she had ever worked for anyone: her debt was enormous.

Waiting for Najima, Celeste could not stop rubbing her eyes, which felt as if they'd been sprinkled with Jadali sand. She'd spent the night communing with Netscape Navigator, tracking down information about *kafala*, human trafficking, and treatment of women in Jadal, filling a notebook with details. Sometime between the second and third pots of coffee, she was able to confirm what Flora had told them: a slave who bore her owner's son could not be sold, and the son would become the owner's heir. Najima could indeed be in danger.

Moreover, it wasn't safe for any of the girls to go back to Jadal: the government would not intervene if a father or brother executed them for dishonoring the family. Most girls were shot or stabbed, though one was drowned in the family swimming pool while her siblings watched. Female crimes included logging onto the web, talking to a boy on the phone, riding in a car with a male who was not a family member. Everyone would assume the maids were wanton: they had lived unmarried in a house with men who were not relatives. And if their families didn't punish them, the government would: single women alone were considered prostitutes and treated accordingly. Some were committed to workhouses, where life was no better than slavery. Celeste realized that she—and, hopefully, Elaine and Abby—not only had to rescue the other maids in the Farouqi household; they had to figure out a future for them. These girls could never go home.

As Najima crept down the stairs toward the kitchen, she was sidetracked by a large room with books lining the walls. All in English, of course, but she couldn't resist running a wistful hand over their spines, then plucking one from the oversized stack on the bottom. She let it fall open. Then she just stared. Was she looking at a picture of Paradise? It was familiar yet foreign, dark and bright at the same time, a night full of brilliant light. She recognized the moon and stars, yet they looked utterly alien: they seemed to vibrate and spin—you could see lines of whirling air, greens and blues and golden yellows, yet who could see air? And the mountains in the distance, the village tucked in the corner, the tall undulating trees—all strange yet familiar, beautiful yet disturbing. She was sure the English text explained everything, if only she could read it.

Zainab had taught her to read before the slave-trader came —it was a secret skill passed down among the women of their family—but the only Arabic books she had access to belonged to the children. She'd read them all many times, but not aloud. It somehow seemed important to conceal her ability—it gave her a tiny scrap of power that the Farouqis would surely take away if they knew. The family didn't read much beyond newspapers and, of course, The Judgments. Najima, who lived impoverished in the midst of great wealth, could scarcely imagine how it would feel to own so many beautiful books. To be able to read any of them, anytime she chose!

"There you are!" Mrs. Flora had found her. "I thought I heard you come down."

Swiftly, Najima closed the book on the beautiful-terrifying night sky and slid it back onto the stack.

"You can look at any of the books," Mrs. Flora reassured her, but habitual guilt, like furtiveness, was not so easy to shake off.

Mrs. Flora led her into the kitchen, where Mrs. Celeste waited. They told her to sit and gave her a cup of tea with sage in it, just like home. Then she was given fruit, milk, toast, eggs, and more tea. It was overwhelming. The women kept urging her to eat. But as soon as she filled her stomach, she jumped up, took her plates to the sink—would Mrs. Celeste mind if they touched?— and began to wash them.

Mrs. Flora said: "No, *habibti*," and Mrs. Celeste actually took the sponge out of her hands.

Najima summoned the few English words she'd picked up from hearing the children's lessons. "I work. Clean big."

Mrs. Celeste shook her head and Mrs. Flora said: "No, you are not a servant here, Najima. You are a guest."

Mrs. Celeste reached out to lay her fingertips against Najima's rounded belly. "Najima and *tefl*," she said. *Tefl* meant baby— Mrs. Flora must have told her the word. "*Duyuf.* Guests."

Najima looked from one to the other. She had no idea what a guest's duties might be.

The moment Benny appeared, Celeste sent him back out with a long shopping list for clothing and toiletries, familiar Middle Eastern foods, an English-Arabic dictionary for herself, and an Arabic-English dictionary for Najima. She hoped the girl could read.

She had not been prepared for the rush of tenderness that swept through her when she saw the girl hesitate at the kitchen door. Najima was a stranger—a foreign, pregnant stranger—yet the mix of fear, bewilderment, and hope on her face reminded Celeste that she was also a child. Najima had experienced and witnessed atrocities, yet, unless too little sleep and too much caffeine was making Celeste imagine things, there was something pure about her. Untainted. The monsters hadn't stolen her soul.

Celeste didn't know which of them was more surprised when, following instinct, she pressed a kiss to Najima's forehead before she left the house.

Elaine and Abby were waiting at the botanical gardens. Linking arms with them so she could keep her voice low, Celeste described the events of the night before. Elaine listened in grim silence, but Abby kept uttering squeals of horror—Celeste had to remind her that they didn't want to attract attention. Nor did she spare her friends the details of her research.

"The births of Jadali male children are recorded, but there are no records for female births," she continued, pulling out her notebook. "Midwives apologize if the baby is a girl; the family expresses sorrow. Even before the umbilical cord is cut, the new mother might get a slap in the face for birthing a female. In the cities, Jadali OB's don't tell a woman the gender of her fetus after a sonogram: they've found women cope better with labor if they don't know it's a girl."

"That is unreal," Elaine muttered.

They were strolling the indoor paths, breathing in the humid air, looking at the familiar greens and blooms without seeing them. Somewhere water dripped. Water always dripped somewhere in London.

"Oh, it's real," Celeste replied. "In some areas, the sale of zucchini and cucumbers to women is banned because authorities think it gives them lewd ideas. Some authorities consider the female voice arousing and forbid women to speak in mixed groups unless they put a stone in their mouth to distort the sound."

"And this—what's the girl's name again?" said Elaine.

"Najima."

"Najima is an actual slave? As in bought-and-paid-for?"

"Not only her. Three other young maids, teenagers. And that's just the Farouqi house. There are about forty words in Arabic for 'slave.'"

Abby shook her head. "Hard to believe. In 1996."

Elaine halted. "The real question is: what are we going to do about it?"

Gratitude rushed through Celeste like adrenalin. Her friends were in this with her—she didn't even need to ask. "We've got to get those girls out of there. They're being molested and abused."

"And they're not even officially here," Elaine mused. "No documents, no records. Private jet. They can't just walk out."

"And even if they could," said Abby, "where would they go? They don't speak English. They don't have money."

"They're trapped," Celeste agreed.

"Doesn't the UK have laws against this kind of thing?" Abby demanded.

"Yes," said Celeste, her voice scratchy. "But they're hard to enforce. I read that the UN's tried putting pressure on members to get them to address the problem, but you know how that goes."

"Committees," said Elaine. "Exploring. Investigating. People talking endlessly without moving their jaws."

"They might get better results if they enforced sanctions against nations that tolerate slavery, but I guess they don't want to use up their political capital." She scanned her notes again. "Private corporations could exert some pressure, urge their boards not to do business with any entity that supports slavery. I'm sure some human rights groups are trying that."

"And look how far they've gotten," Elaine pointed out.

"But do we really want to interfere with their culture? Isn't this something the police should handle?" asked Abby.

Now Celeste came to a halt. "Abby. That woman was kicking a pregnant girl in the stomach."

"Anyway, what can the police do?" said Elaine. "They're not going to risk causing an international incident when they don't have any hard evidence. They don't have any legal grounds to search the house."

That's right," said Celeste. She stopped again and looked at her friends. "It has to be us. *We're* all they've got."

"But what about the boys?" said Abby. "Their deal with the sheik? Ted will never forgive me if we ruin it."

"We have to be damn careful," said Celeste.

"We have to be damn sneaky," said Elaine. "But we can't just storm the citadel. We need more information—a reconnaissance mission. How can we get back inside?"

"My jacket," Celeste said with grim satisfaction. "I left it there when I hustled Najima out. I still have the ticket in my bag."

"You can call them," said Elaine. "Ask if you can drop by."

"We'll come with you," said Abby.

"Wouldn't that look odd, the three of us traveling in a pack? As if we were scared?"

"I *am* scared," said Abby.

"Take Flora," said Elaine. "Don't let on that she speaks Arabic. Maybe they'll drop some clues."

Celeste squeezed her friend's arm. "Brilliant!"

She took a deep breath of warm damp air and paused to study a pink ruffled orchid. Orchids always reminded her of her favorite artist's flower paintings, which—no matter how Georgia O'Keefe protested—inevitably called to mind the essence of a woman: the depth, the delicate folds and ridges, the sense of peering into a secret. And she thought about the research she had *not* shared with Abby and Elaine: the accounts of tribal female circumcision, performed just before puberty. Girls were held down by their mothers and sisters and aunts for this procedure. When they married, they had to be penetrated with great force. Some tribes erected special "honeymoon tents" at a far enough distance so the bride's screams would not disturb the others.

Celeste did not believe in condemning other people's religious convictions, but she also did not believe in mutilating genitalia and depriving women of sexual pleasure. Beyond the physical suffering, it seemed like desecration—a strike against life itself. She imagined bringing Najima here, showing her all the greenery and brilliant blooms. "*This* is what you are," she would tell her. "Not someone's property." There were so many wonders she could introduce Najima to when it was safe: the parks, the river, the *ocean*. The great city itself, its canyons and towers. Double-decker buses. Belgian chocolate crepes. And it *would* be safe. They would rescue those girls. Even if it did cause an international incident.

Hurrying to catch up with Elaine and Abby, she announced: "All right, then. We may be a bunch of frivolous old bags with too much money and too much leisure, but that's going to work in our favor."

"How?" asked Abby.

Celeste grinned. She was definitely feeling better. "They'll never see us coming."

CHAPTER THREE

B y the next day, arrangements were made. Celeste and a "dear friend" would visit *Hadiqa House* to pick up the jacket and take coffee with the two Mesdames Farouqi. Flora—the dear friend—had agreed instantly to the masquerade: she had a surprising taste for mischief, and it was a chance to do a service for those girls, poor souls. Elaine and Abby came to stay with Najima, who clutched her new Arab-English dictionary, already showing wear. The girl had been overwhelmed by the load of new clothes and toiletries that Benny heaped in her arms.

"Shukran, shukran, Mrs. Benny!" she kept saying, puzzled when everyone laughed.

Flora explained that Najima should call them by their first names, as they did her.

Najima frowned. "Mrs. Flora." It was not a question. "Mrs. Celeste."

Celeste shook her head. "Just Celeste," she said, touching her chest as she'd done the night they met.

Flora explained in Arabic: "She is saying you are equal: you are created from the same earth."

Najima studied Celeste's face, something she wouldn't have dared to do two days ago. Then she looked at Flora: "I am created from the same earth, but I am not equal because I have never gone to school."

When Flora translated, Celeste said: "Then you shall go to school. Tell her, Flora." Then she added: "No, wait," and flipped through her English-Arabic dictionary till she found the words herself. "*Madrasa*. School. *Waead.* Promise."

"Close enough," said Flora. "Atrocious accent."

But Najima understood. She reached for Celeste's hands and bent over them, touching her forehead.

No one required a translation.

Meanwhile, Myrtle the midwife had examined Najima and pronounced her, aside from being underfed, in reasonably good shape. She prescribed vitamins, folic acid, iron, magnesium, and lots of milk, all of which Benny rushed out to get. She also trimmed the girl's ragged tufts of hair and promised to look in every few days.

Flora, a skilled cook who had managed to recreate some of Celeste's childhood favorites—from matzoh balls and kugel to chalupas and chili—had long since mastered Middle Eastern cuisine. She cooked chicken with rice and pine nuts, eggplant-tomato stew, fava beans with lamb—all dishes Najima greeted with delight. Flora kept filling her plate until the girl declared: "I am stuffed to the chin!"

Then it was her turn, Flora translating, to brief the ladies on the tastes and habits of the Farouqi women: Begum and Mehraj, like most wealthy Jadali matrons, slept till noon, then filled the hours with phone calls, dressing up, visiting friends, shopping, and having lunch at restaurants the sheik had pre-approved. In London they were also addicted to the doctors in Harley Street, going often for tests and consultations. Flora added that some ladies had plastic surgery every time they visited the West. Since this was frowned upon in Jadal, they had to invent excuses: a nose job became a nose broken in a car accident and repaired. An eyelid-tuck became a wonderful new face cream that performed miracles. A breast-lift was a new bra engineered with amazing support. No doubt Begum and Mehraj, who were not often visited by Western ladies, would be taking extra pains with their appearance today: lots of make-up, jewelry, the latest couture.

Najima said that Flora and Celeste should also dress to impress—anything less would be considered an insult.

Flora reminded Celeste not to touch anyone, eat with her left hand, accept more than three refills, or discuss religion, adding: "And it's a deadly insult to throw a shoe."

"For heaven's sake!" said Celeste. "Why would I throw a shoe?"

"Or cross your legs. If you expose the sole of your foot, that's just as bad."

Abby and Elaine put together Donna Karan outfits from Celeste's closet—power clothes for the woman executive. Since Flora was shorter, Abby helped her roll the waistline and tape the hem, which had them all giggling like teenagers. Even Najima smiled. Elaine applied their make-up—Willow, of course—with a heavy hand so they would fit in.

When they were ready, Celeste had to remind Flora to get in the back seat with her instead of up front with Benny. "And remember," she said, "you don't understand Arabic. Don't let anything show on your face."

"Not to worry, Mrs. C," Flora replied. "I've had more practice than you could possibly imagine."

By daylight the house shone blindingly white in the dull London winter, taking up an entire city block. Celeste hadn't realized that the tall stucco walls enclosing the compound were quite so formidable. No wonder the girls needed outside help to escape.

"Stay close but out of sight, Benny," she murmured as a uniformed servant opened the car door.

"Yes, Missus," he replied, adding: "You two look after yourselves."

Celeste realized he must be worried about Flora and felt a twinge of guilt for involving others in what had been her own rash decision. Then she remembered Najima curled up on the floor, Begum's foot poised to kick her in the stomach. No, she really hadn't had any other choice.

The servant escorted them up the grand stairs to the women's reception room, where the ladies of the house awaited at opposite ends of a white velvet couch. As Najima had predicted, they were formally dressed, crisp and tailored. They would have looked like they were attending a business meeting if not for all the necklaces, bangles, and rings.

Celeste introduced Flora—Mrs. Butters—and they were greeted politely, if not warmly, and given a once-over their hosts did not bother to disguise. Celeste felt as if they were examining her credentials. She was glad she'd decided on Donna Karan and tried not to sneeze at the haze of Strategy hanging over the couch. A very large male servant brought in a tray of cardamom-spiced coffee, which they sipped from tiny glasses rimmed with gold.

Accepting sugar—lots of it—Celeste complimented the two Mrs. Farouqis on the success of the gala and the beauty of their new house. She hoped it wasn't rude to turn in her chair and openly survey the reception room.

"Such an unusual blend of styles," she said.

"My husband choose every thing," Mehraj said in careful English.

"Did he really?" Celeste took in the ornate lamps and mirrors, gilded side tables, claw-footed consoles, and white tiger skin rugs. She was groping for something more to say about the décor when Flora stepped in to save her:

"Won't you tell us about your children, Madam Farouqi?" she asked. It was exactly the right question, as Flora well knew.

Of course, there were two Mesdames Farouqis, but Tariq was hardly a child, so Mehraj chattered happily about her little girls. "They learn English now—very smart girls. But—" she patted her belly delicately, "next time, a son. *Inshallah.*"

Begum shot her a black look and muttered something in Arabic, also ending with *Inshallah.* Celeste hoped Flora had caught it. She wondered how much English the older wife understood. But the pat on the belly reminded her of Najima and their mission. Best get on with it. As soon as the oversized manservant refilled her glass, she steeled herself and tipped it, allowing hot coffee to spill down her front. Another outfit ruined. Perhaps this could be her new party trick.

She jumped up, dabbing at her chest with the napkin. The other women all exclaimed in alarm, but Celeste laughed it off. "I am just so clumsy!" Her dormant Texas accent was emerging. "Big hands, teeny-tiny glass. If I could just visit the little girls' room…?"

There was a moment's confusion about what "little girls' room" meant—not Mehraj's daughters after all—then the servant led Celeste down the hall to a lavish powder room. He looked rather sullen—perhaps he resented babysitter duty? She dawdled, running the water, dabbing the stain. Then she cracked the door open. He was waiting down the hall, his massive back turned. Giving her privacy or blocking her escape? Easing the door shut so he would think her still inside, she stole off in the opposite direction, shoes in hand. For the second time, she was sneaking around *Hadiqa House* on her own. Silently she repeated the girls' names: Fadeelah. Jameela. Dafiya. She wanted to find them. She wanted to see their faces and show them hers, somehow let them know that the cavalry was coming.

More open doors, more possibilities. Like a cat burglar, she sidled up to each one, peering carefully inside. Somewhere a television played. Most of the rooms were sumptuous but empty, each wife assigned her own spacious apartments. Then she heard the muted bang of filing cabinet drawers slamming shut. Someone in a hurry. Following the sound, she risked a glance into a luxurious office: huge desk, plush leather, formal photos of the Jadali king and crown prince on the walls. Touches of gold everywhere. Even the filing cabinet handles were gold. Did the sheik fancy himself King Midas?

She was just in time to see Tariq yanking a fat folder from the cabinet drawer with apparent glee, then jamming it into his briefcase, which he locked shut. He tested the lock three times— whatever was in there was that important.

As soon as this registered, Celeste realized she had actually stepped over the threshold. Tariq looked up. She was caught.

"Is your husband with you?" he asked abruptly.

The question seemed odd. "Ex-husband," she said. "And no. I forgot my jacket the other night and your mother was kind enough to invite me for coffee, which I spilled on my blouse—"

Tariq's gaze dropped to her chest—deliberately, she thought. He was trying to fluster her, put her on the defensive: he didn't think she was capable of playing offense. But Celeste was from Texas. She knew how to be offensive. Time to put the Primary Principle into action.

"—so, after I cleaned up, I'm afraid I succumbed to curiosity and wandered off on my own," she continued smoothly. "But Mr. Farouqi, I thought you had your own flat and offices in town."

"I do. I was looking for some papers my father has misplaced."

"So, you work for him?"

The question seemed to annoy him. "We are partners in the family enterprises, but I also have business interests of my own —a nightclub, for instance, which you and your friends must visit as my guests. In the special room for VIPs, of course."

Trying to flatter her. This young man was fearless. Easy to be fearless when you are born into money, then spend your life watching money reproduce itself. Simpering middle-aged women probably fell like leaves when he turned on the charm. But Najima had too many bruises for Celeste to be affected by charm.

"And business is good?" Not a polite question in British society, but, after all, she was just a crass American.

"Oh, indeed. Business is booming." A private smile crossed Tariq's face, but he didn't share the joke.

They regarded each other for a moment. In his pressed black jeans and snakeskin boots, Tariq looked as elegant as he had in a tuxedo. So, what was off about him? He was handsome enough. Was his head truly too big for his body? Did he seem like a man who should have been taller? Should have been something? What was it?

Before she could probe further, he continued: "But where are my manners? Since you are interested in the house, you must allow me to give you a tour." He crooked his elbow for her to take. His other hand tightened on the briefcase.

She had no choice—to refuse would seem hostile. Besides, perhaps this way she could still collect the information she needed.

"Very kind, thank you," she said, dropping her shoes and stuffing her feet into them. She took his arm gingerly. "But could we include my friend Flora? She's still visiting with your mother. Mothers." Damn it, she didn't know which was correct.

That private smile again. "Of course."

He locked the office door behind them, then tested it. Twice.

Tariq found the other woman chatting with Mehraj in the reception room, mostly about children. Begum looked disgruntled. This was not her favorite subject. Tariq had been keeping an eye on Mehraj, watching her belly. She and Muhktar were trying for a son, which did not suit Tariq at all. Lately he'd been reading up on SIDS. Fascinating phenomenon, and no one to blame. God's will.

Begum's face eased when she saw Tariq, although he could tell she did not like him touching the *Amreekiyah*. No matter. In the West, you adopted Western ways. It lulled people into thinking you were like them.

"Ladies, would you care to join us on a tour of Hadiqa House?" he said.

"Yes please," said Flora, jumping up. "That would be lovely."

Begum glanced at Flora. "What is she?" she asked Tariq in Arabic.

He knew exactly what she meant. "My guess would be Malaysian or Filipina. Excellent investments—little brown sex machines. Much cheaper than Japanese women and they'll do whatever you like."

Celeste did not know what they were saying, but she saw

Flora stiffen, then deliberately relax.

"When are you going to replace the one who ran?" Begum asked Tariq.

He shrugged. "I'll send my man back out. It shouldn't take long."

"Tell him to get two. Tell him to find uglier ones."

Tariq turned to the others and switched to English. "But we are neglecting our guests. Shall we begin the tour?"

He stuck his other elbow out for Flora to take, but she pretended not to see. Only Celeste caught the scathing glance she sent his way.

"We'll start with the men's reception room," Tariq said, leading them out to the corridor. He knew his mother would like him to cut the visit short, but he needed more time to observe the Stoneman woman. There was something off about her. Sneaking around the house with her shoes in her hand? What game was she playing?

It crossed his mind that she could be a spy, working for the police or even a rival cartel, but she didn't seem bright enough for that. Still, using a middle-aged matron would be brilliant camouflage. Could she be spying on behalf of her ex-husband? Something to do with the pipe deal? He clenched the briefcase handle a bit tighter. Unlikely. Still, he wanted to study her a bit more.

"Such interesting style," she said as they entered the great room. "I hear that your father chose everything himself?"

Tariq frowned. The words were respectful enough, but something about the tone. Was she mocking him? Mocking them?

"Yes," he replied, "we did engage a design firm, but he rejected all their ideas. So, they took him round to private warehouses where he selected whatever caught his eye."

Celeste took in the classic Chesterfield sofas, Louis XV consoles, and Baroque-framed mirrors. At least the rich smell of leather managed to subdue the lingering stink of Strategy. Celeste and Flora toured the room, murmuring continuous appreciation and noting the inordinate number of horse sculptures—all fierce rearing stallions like the ones that encircled the fountain outside.

"I've heard about legendary *Bedu* horsemanship," Celeste said. "These are impressive."

Tariq pounced. "The average Westerner says Bedouin. How do you come to know the correct term, Mrs. Stoneman?"

Celeste saw his eyes narrow. Did he suspect something? After all, a girl was missing. "Maybe I'm just not your average Westerner, Mr. Farouqi. And you used the term the other night, at the gala."

Flora gave a snort, quickly disguised as a cough.

Tariq's easy smile returned. "Do you see these?" He pointed to a pair of crossed scimitars on the wall. "They are the real thing, not props from the sword dance."

The curved scimitars indeed looked ancient. And sharp.

"We have a saying in my homeland," Tariq continued. *"I against my brother. I and my brother against my cousins. I and my cousins against the world."*

Celeste noticed that he didn't mention fathers or sons. "Very tribal," she said.

"Indeed. Shall we examine some of the antiquities?"

He led them down the stairs to the glass cases lining the corridor. "Some of these go back to the sixth century. This, for example—" he pointed to a gilded elephant clock. "It was powered by a hidden water system and metal balls that dropped. It would still work today if we set it up. And this is an astrolabe."

They peered at the disk with its pivoted pointer and edge marked in degrees.

"A navigation instrument?" Celeste guessed.

"Also astronomical. Used for finding directions, telling time, observing the universe. This one goes back three thousand years."

Celeste gazed down at star maps in faded blue and gold, allowing herself a brief pang—Abby and Elaine would have really appreciated these things. But this was a mission, not a social call.

"You are aware, of course, that it took the Egyptians, Chinese, Indians, and Greeks a thousand years to discover what my people already knew," Tariq continued. "Mathematics, astronomy, encryption, navigation, engineering—we had windmills five hundred years before the Dutch even heard of them."

"I've read that the *Bedu* invented genealogy to give themselves a sense of continuity," said Celeste.

That word again. Tariq gave her a sharp glance. Was she taunting him? Implying she knew more than she was saying?

"Yes," he replied smoothly. "We are an exceedingly clever people."

Celeste tried to read his face. Was this authentic pride in his heritage? Or a form of one-upmanship?

"I'm sure you're aware that we invented the common number system," he went on. "And we invented geometry from the study of angles."

Celeste was pretty sure that Euclid had invented geometry, but she said nothing.

"I understand that English-speakers also use 'angle' in a different way" Tariq went on. His smile was vaguely disturbing. "If someone has an angle, he is playing some sort of…what is the word…con? Is that right, Mrs. Stoneman?"

"Not necessarily a con, Mr. Farouqi. It could also be an agenda, a point-of-view, a cause. Even a righteous cause."

"Is that so? My father would approve. I prefer to think of it as a game."

Was he trying to send her a message? Or did he always sound as if he was alluding to some private joke? *I and myself against everyone else.*

"Some of these cases are empty," she remarked. "Weren't there more artifacts out the other night?"

"You are observant, Mrs. Stoneman. Some of these objects are fine museum-quality replications, but others are priceless antiques. We display them on special occasions but keep them permanently in a vault. I call it the Treasure Room." He raised his eyebrows. "Would you like to see?"

"Oh, very much," Celeste replied, though she would have liked even more to smack the patronizing smile off his face.

"Come. We'll take the lift." He grinned. "It is a paradox: in this house, one must go up to go down."

Puzzled, they followed him up the stairs and down the hall to a large room crammed with toys: dolls, stuffed animals, games, blocks, tricycles. Two little girls, perhaps three and five, in matching pink dresses and ruffled socks, sprawled on cushions, watching a Disney video. They turned to gaze at the strangers with huge dark eyes, the smaller girl sucking her finger. Celeste smiled at them, glad there were some Farouqis she could like without reservation.

Everyone turned when an interior door opened and out came the wraith Celeste had seen rushing away when Begum was beating Najima. She again held an infant wrapped in a pink blanket. Stopping short when she saw the visitors, she stammered something in Arabic, looking anxiously from Begum to Mehraj.

This time Tariq was good enough to translate. "Fadeelah says she only left the girls for a second to change the baby's nappie." He turned a wry smile on the visitors. "You must forgive us—we are short-handed at the moment. We've just lost a staff-member. Most unexpected."

Did Celeste imagine that his gaze lingered on her face?

Mehraj took the baby, folding back the blanket so Celeste and Flora could see.

"Third girl," she said and repeated: "But soon a son, *inshallah*."

Celeste made appropriate cooing sounds but kept one eye on Tariq. His expression had flickered when Mehraj mentioned a son. Flora was right. This was a dangerous young man.

Celeste tried to catch Fadeelah's eye, but the maid's eyes were fixed on Begum. "Oh, is that a balcony?" she asked instead, stalling.

Obligingly, Tariq opened the French doors so they could step into the cold air. "All the private rooms have balconies. It is how we bring the garden inside."

"Of course," Celeste murmured. "*Hadiqa House*."

She looked down at flagstones, bare branches, empty flower beds. It would all be very picturesque in spring. Too bad the maids weren't allowed to enjoy it. Staff-member, Tariq had said. Why not call a slave a slave?

When the baby began to fuss, Begum barked something at the maid. You didn't need to speak Arabic to understand.

"And now the Treasure Room," Tariq announced, opening the door to a large closet lined with shelves crammed with more toys. At first Celeste thought he was joking. Then, to her astonishment, he took hold of a middle shelf and pulled. The entire wall of shelves swung out, revealing the sleek steel doors of a concealed elevator. Lift.

"We don't make it easy for thieves," Tariq said as he inserted a key. The doors slid silently open. "Ladies."

Begum and Mehraj stayed behind. Presumably, they had seen enough treasure.

The doors opened in the basement, which was more of a warehouse, stacked with large crates and bulky objects covered in tarps. Lights blinked on and security monitors flashed till they came to an intimidating steel door guarded by an enormous cobra encased in glass, hood fully flared, fangs exposed, ready to strike.

Celeste halted abruptly and forgot not to invoke the Lord: "Holy God, it's real!"

"Was," Tariq corrected her. "It's been taxidermized, but I assure you it's quite dead." Then, seeing their faces, he laughed. "It does look alive, doesn't it? My father's idea—a guardian to discourage any curiosity about what's beyond the door. We have a very superstitious staff."

"I'm feeling pretty superstitious myself at the moment," Celeste muttered.

"If you wouldn't mind looking away while I punch in the code?" Tariq asked, busy with the door's digital lock.

It was not really a question. Flora and Celeste turned around until they heard the great door unlatch.

"Ladies," said Tariq.

They had to step up and over a raised threshold. "It's like entering a bomb shelter," said Celeste, remembering the air raid drills of her youth.

"Actually, the vault is bomb-proof," said Tariq. "Also, waterproof and fireproof, with state-of-the-art climate control. You may find it chilly."

The vault was freezing, its walls lined with pullout drawers like safety-deposit boxes and weighty steel cases containing the treasures. A transparent window of some unbreakable material revealed the contents of each case, from scientific instruments to primitive pottery. Everything was numbered and labeled. Tariq, making notes in the security log, pointed out the humidity, light, temperature, ventilation, and air controls attached to the alarm system—he seemed more proud of those than of the antiquities themselves.

"I guess it could double as a panic room," Celeste said.

"I don't need a panic room," Tariq replied. "I have scimitars."

It was impossible to tell whether he was joking. And it was probably absurd to fear that he might step out, slam the great door, and trap them inside. Still, she did not move far from the threshold, instead turning slowly in place to survey the vault, when something odd caught her eye. It was an all-too-familiar shape, an item she'd become intimately acquainted with during her ten years in London. What was an umbrella doing in a waterproof vault? It looked like an ordinary black umbrella, every Englishman's appendage, with a stout handle and long shiny tip. But something bothered her, something didn't look quite right, though she couldn't pin it down. She couldn't risk asking questions or even staring at the thing too long—Tariq already sensed something squirrely about her—but she fixed the image in her mind to think about later.

After they returned to the ground floor, Celeste texted Benny, and Tariq walked them to the door, where Begum and Mehraj waited to say goodbye. But before anyone could speak, there was a flurry of activity outside, and the guards snapped to attention. The door opened to admit a man Celeste didn't recognize for a moment. It was the sheik, wearing an exquisite silk suit, shirt, and tie, all handmade, she guessed. Yet he seemed so ordinary, compared to the way he'd looked in his robes, that Celeste wondered whether he deliberately used the robes as camouflage, so you noticed them more than the man within.

Muhktar did seem distracted as he greeted them—no longer the serene and gracious host of the gala but a harried businessman. He spoke in English out of courtesy to the visitors but directed his words to Tariq.

"The contract?" he asked.

Tariq shook his head. "I went through every drawer. No sign of it."

Celeste caught her breath. She distinctly remembered seeing Tariq shove a folder into his briefcase, then test the briefcase's lock. He was still clutching that briefcase—he had not put it down once, as if it were handcuffed to his wrist.

Muhktar seemed distressed. That meant he might be vulnerable. Celeste decided to push her luck: she might not get another chance. "I understand one of your staff has gone missing," she said, aware of Tariq's sharp glance. "Do you think she ran away?"

"We have not yet learned where she has gone," Muhktar replied, a non-answer worthy of a politician.

"Do you need help? We know people at the Metropolitan Police, or what you might call Scotland Yard..." This was a lie, but she wanted to see his reaction.

Najima's rapist, always formal, stiffened. "Thank you but no. It is an internal matter."

"But the poor girl might be in danger—does she know anyone in London? Does she speak any English?"

Muhktar's voice became even more wooden. "Thank you, but

this is a family matter. A Jadali matter." For another man, that might have been a conclusive rebuff, but Muhktar seemed to swell inside his well-cut suit: he had more to say. "As the giver of commands, I must claim my duty and responsibility to govern those in my care. Everyone has a place, and they must keep to it for their own good and the good of the household. They might cry and complain, but their souls will thank me for helping them be what God intended."

For once Celeste was speechless. Flora spared her from having to respond to this extraordinary statement by announcing brightly: "Here's Benny!"

Goodbyes and thanks were exchanged in English and Arabic. No hands were shaken but heads were inclined. Celeste and Flora had almost made it through the door when Tariq called: "Wait!" and Celeste thought the jig was up.

"I believe this is yours, Mrs. Stoneman?" said Tariq, taking her leather jacket from one of the servants. "After all, it's what you came for, is it not?"

The glint in his eye told Celeste that he was just as aware of their cat-and-mouse game as she was. She accepted the jacket without a word, smiling blandly.

Then at last she and Flora were scrambling into the car. As Benny pulled away from the house, Celeste said: "Tell me."

Flora's goodbye-and-thank-you smile vanished. "Mrs. C," she said grimly, "it's a viper pit. We've got to get those girls out."

CHAPTER FOUR

The full debriefing had to wait until the team was back together, sitting around Celeste's kitchen table, eating sandwiches Abby had made and drinking Flora's blistering hot tea. Celeste and Flora were ravenous: espionage turned out to be hard work. Between bites, Flora translated for Najima, who ate with her new dictionary parked on her lap. Abby and Elaine had spent the morning teaching her so many English words that she had acquired a handy new tool — "What mins?"—which she employed as often as possible.

Celeste began by repeating what Mehraj had said about hoping for a son. She asked if Flora had heard Begum's muttered response.

"Yes. She said: *May your womb shrivel like a dried onion.* It's one of the worst possible Arab curses."

She repeated the Arabic for Najima, who gasped. Celeste felt a little rattled herself. What a thing to wish on someone who wanted a child! But it fit the expression on Tariq's face when Mehraj repeated her hopes in the nursery. Begum and her son clearly agreed on this score. The two of them were a danger not only to Najima but to any male child Mehraj might have.

"What else did Begum say?" she asked.

"In the nursery, she called Fadeelah a she-goat, a whore, and a lazy dog. But the worst thing—" Flora paused. "I'm not sure I can say it."

Celeste found this alarming—Flora had always seemed utterly imperturbable.

Benny covered Flora's hand with his. "Whisper in my ear, pet."

Flora shook her head. This was not something she wanted to say in front of her husband. This was not something she wanted to say at all. But no point in being missish: real lives were on the line. Squeezing Benny's fingers, she began: "Begum asked Tariq what I am."

"*What* you are?" said Celeste.

"Yes. Those two see people as whats. Tariq said he guessed I was Malaysian or Filipina, calling us excellent investments." Flora hesitated, but there was no way around it and she was no coward. "He said we were little brown sex machines. That we were better than Japanese women because we're cheaper and don't wear out as fast."

"In front of his mother?" Abby gasped, nearly drowned out by Benny's outraged "Bugger me!"

"Buk-armee," Najima repeated carefully. "What mins?"

Flora, not entirely displeased by Benny's reaction, put one calming hand on his arm and another on Najima's. "But what happened next is more important," she continued. "Begum asked when he was going to replace Najima. He said he'd send his man back out. Begum told him to get two and to find uglier ones."

"Dear God," said Celeste.

"He's a trafficker," Elaine said.

"They all are. The whole family is complicit," said Flora. "The entire culture looks the other way, along with every nation that does business with them."

Celeste shook her head. "All true. But Tariq is something more."

She described their encounter: how Tariq stuffed a file into his briefcase and later lied to Muhktar about it, how he immediately demanded to know whether Neil had come with Celeste—

"Why would he care about Neil?" Abby interrupted.

"Could have something to do with the pipe deal," Elaine mused.

"Muhktar did say contract. Tariq said he couldn't find it, but..."

Elaine tapped a finger on the table. "You don't suppose he's trying to screw his father out of the deal, do you?"

"I would have no trouble supposing any such thing," Celeste retorted. "But how would that work?"

"If he set up shell companies and used them to underbid the boys, he could steal the contract without Muhktar ever knowing who was behind it."

"The flash bastard," muttered Benny. "Probably drinks his own bathwater."

"Bass-a-ter," Najima repeated. "What mins?"

Flora patted her arm.

"But why cheat his father?" Abby asked. "They're both rich as Croesus."

"For the same reason he won't tolerate a brother," Elaine snapped. "He doesn't want to settle for his share—he wants it all."

"Ego too," Celeste added. "He'd love the chance to out-sheik the sheik."

"Sheik." Najima nodded grimly. This word she knew.

"Should we warn the boys?" Abby asked.

"Not yet," said Celeste. "That's not our main concern right now." She described the other disturbing aspects of the visit— the hints Tariq dropped, the veiled intimidation, the snake, the Treasure Room. Suddenly she remembered what had bothered her in the vault. "The umbrella! There was an umbrella in there. A perfectly ordinary umbrella. But what would it be doing in a vault?"

Elaine, refilling everyone's cup, pointed out the obvious: "It must not be ordinary."

Celeste shut her eyes, fixing the memory. "It looked brand-new. And there was something about the tip—a little too long, a little too pointy."

"He's up to something," said Flora. "Besides smuggling girls."

"He's up to a lot of things," Elaine said. "Richard says the

Farouqis are in bed with the royal family—kickbacks, bribes, access to slush funds. I wonder how they'd stand up to a forensic audit."

"If Tariq has secret income streams, he must have ways of laundering the money," said Celeste. "That nightclub, I bet. At least."

"Jadalis are very proper, very private," Flora warned. "They take offense at even the suggestion of corruption."

Celeste shook her head. "Well, regardless, that's still not our focus at the moment. We need to find a way to get those girls out."

Benny thumped the table with his fist. Najima flinched. "Let me and my mates have a go," he growled.

"Enough of that," Flora scolded. "You're scaring the girl."

Benny tucked his hands out of sight, looking so contrite that Najima smiled.

"Besides," Flora added, "you're outnumbered. They've got a private army."

Abby brought them back to the question. "So, what can we do?"

Everyone turned to stare at Celeste, who stared at them, then abruptly shoved back her chair. "Let's go wake up the Answer Box," she said and led the way to her computer.

After an hour of pointing and clicking, combining search terms, and leaping from link to link, Celeste had to admit defeat. The Answer Box just did not have what they needed. Abby, who had been taking diligent notes, read the results aloud: according to Netscape Navigator, they could research (or write!) software to detect money laundering; they could lobby for stock/mutual fund divestment campaigns to defund entities who profited from human trafficking; they could demand that the U.N. appoint an Anti-Slavery Ambassador and establish an inspection mandate; they could petition the Queen.

Celeste turned off the computer. None of these well-intended suggestions was going to get those girls out of that house or prevent new ones from replacing them.

"We've got to do it ourselves," she said. "Somehow."

"Anyone got a rocket launcher?" asked Elaine.

Benny spoke up. "We can watch," he said. "My mates and me—we're all drivers; there's always limos cruising through that neighborhood; we won't attract attention if we take turns."

Flora nodded. "Good idea."

"I'll draw up a schedule, talk to the lads. At least we'll have eyes on the house."

"Good," said Celeste. "I guess the only other thing is to try the police."

"I thought you said they couldn't help," said Abby.

"Not with the evidence we had before, but given what Flora heard..." She sighed. "I didn't want to involve you all, and I especially didn't want to expose Najima, but I don't think we have any choice. They'll probably want to talk to everyone. If I can get their attention."

"That may take a while," Elaine said.

Benny grinned. "I put my money on you, Missus."

"Well, I'm from Texas," said Celeste. "Bad guys don't win. We'll get those bastards."

"Bass-a-ter," Najima repeated, nodding. She was a fast learner.

For dinner Flora made one of her excellent curries. Afterward, everyone was wiped out, but luckily tonight was Thursday, ER night. Celeste, Abby, and Elaine had become addicted to the American TV show about young doctors running the Emergency Room in a big Chicago hospital. They loved it with such passion, discussing the characters as if they were real people living next door, that, as a joke, Celeste had gone to a uniform supply store and bought each woman her own pair of blue scrubs—she even found the paper shower caps to cover their hair—which they donned ceremoniously to watch their favorite show. It didn't hurt that Thursday was also soccer night for the boys, who gathered at Neil's house to watch the match, slap palms, and drink single-malt older than they were.

Tonight, Flora joined the ladies for ER, presumably to translate for Najima, but Celeste could tell her housekeeper was instantly hooked. George Clooney—the actor who played roguish pediatrician Doug Ross—tended to have that effect. None of the ladies referred to him as Doug: it was always George Clooney, with the appropriate note of awe. His dark eyes and curly grin melted women of all ages, and Flora was no exception. Nor was Najima, who immediately learned to say Shorsh Kaloon-ee whenever he appeared onscreen. Celeste resolved to buy a pair of blue scrubs for the two newest members of the club.

Tonight's episode, entitled "Baby Shower," seemed tailor-made for Najima: it involved eight laboring women being transferred from Maternity to the ER due to a faulty sprinkler system. Najima stared, transfixed, whenever the camera focused on the eight big bellies, and Celeste wondered whether she had imagined her own labor and what would follow. Probably not: serving the Farouqis was like living in prison camp—it left no room to plan a future. During one gory close-up of a delivery, Celeste reached for Najima's hand. The girl glanced at her, surprised, but didn't pull away. It struck Celeste that ER doctors and nurses were ordinary flawed individuals who lived in a state of constant crisis, constant rescue—unheroic people doing heroic things. Was that why she loved the show so much? In addition to George Clooney's grin?

Najima watched the laboring women intently. She had seen women give birth before, but never in a hospital. All the steel, all the white, all the men. She shivered. Where were the women's mothers and aunties? Where, for that matter, were her own? The thought that Zainab would not be with her, might not ever see her first grandchild, made Najima want to cry. Zainab used to say: "Your tears are your jewels—let no one see them," and Najima had been very strong about crying up until now. But something in the last few days had started breaking her down, and her eyes filled.

But then Mrs. Celeste ran to the kitchen during the break and reappeared with a huge bowl of what Najima thought were small, dried flowers. They gave off a warm yellow scent that made her mouth water, despite her tears.

"Popcorn," said Mrs. Celeste, offering the bowl.

"Bub-cor," Najima repeated, watching the other ladies take handfuls. She plucked a single flower from the bowl and set it gingerly on her tongue. Her mouth flooded. The popcorn dissolved, melted but still chewy. The flavor was salty, savory, but not like meat or cheese. Her mouth demanded more. Mrs. Flora grinned, tipped the bowl, and poured a heap into Najima's lap.

"Good?" asked Mrs. Celeste, rubbing her belly.

"Bub-cor good," said Najima, rubbing her own rounded belly. "*Tefl* good."

Mrs. Celeste said something to the others, who laughed. Najima hoped she'd told them that the baby liked popcorn.

Benny, who had been out mobilizing his spy team, returned just as the show ended, bringing yet another exotic treat. This one was cold, its container beaded with moisture. When Mrs. Benny pried off the lid, Najima saw a smooth pink mound studded with red chunks.

"Strawberry," Benny said unnecessarily. "Girls like pink, don't they?"

Mrs. Benny handed out spoons. Najima copied the others, digging her spoon into the container when it came to her. She closed her lips around the spoon, and her mouth exploded with tangy sweet cold.

"Ice cream," said Mrs. Celeste, rubbing her belly again. "Good?"

Everyone was smiling, watching Najima, who patted her own

belly. "*Tefl*. Iss-a-crim. Good!"

They laughed again as she held out her spoon for more.

Afterward, sated with popcorn, ice cream, and Shorsh Ka-loon-ee, Najima washed herself in the elegant bathroom, using the Western toilet with new confidence: her belly was starting to get in the way of squatting, so sitting was easier—you only had to go half as far. Only when she crawled into bed did she notice the book waiting on her nightstand, the same book she'd been looking at yesterday morning. Mrs. Flora must have put it there. In Najima's hands it fell open to the magical picture. Her eyes traveled over every inch of the page. She had never looked at anything so hard, not even her mother's broken fertility goddess. And she wasn't looking just with her eyes: in her mind she could see the soil swirling below just as the skies swirled above. Roots, rocks, earth, stars, the very air trembling, constantly in motion. As if you could see the universe breathing.

Celeste rapped on the open door. Some instinct had drawn her here to look in, to say goodnight. She hadn't expected to find Najima studying an art book, but had anything about the last few days been expected?

Najima instantly turned the book to show her. "What mins?"

Starry Night. Good question. Celeste sat on the bed, took the book, and flipped to the short biographies at the back. She pointed to the photo of van Gogh's famous self-portrait—the one with the furry hat and bandage over his mutilated ear. Then she pulled her dictionary out of her scrubs pocket, riffling till she found the right word.

"*Fannan*," she said. "Artist." She tapped the self-portrait. "Vincent." Then she tapped her own chest— "Celeste"—and Najima's hand: "Najima."

Najima nodded, understanding but unsatisfied. She remembered the night sky in the desert: chips of light scattered across the black like a promise. Yet here in London the sky was opaque, inscrutable. And what of this *fannan*, this Fin-sen? His sky was like no other—rapturous, disturbing, a power all its own. But sky was sky. Wasn't that what she'd been taught? The same truth applied everywhere because the same Creator had made all. Questions she couldn't quite formulate swirled through her head.

She tapped the picture, then pointed out the window where clouds like dark bunched muscles obscured the moon. "What mins?" she asked again.

Celeste, too, looked from book to sky and back. What was the girl asking? Was she talking about artistic vision? Was she asking what was real? What was *true*?

Tears pricked Celeste's eyes. This child moved her in ways she couldn't explain. She had the feeling she was being entrusted with something so precious she was almost afraid to proceed, afraid of making a mistake. This girl had been taught to absorb answers, not ask questions. Celeste lifted her arms in the universal gesture of "Who knows," pointing to her own heart and head, then Najima's, hoping to somehow convey the sense of *this is something everyone must work out for herself*.

Najima traced the swirls on the page with her finger. Then she traced around her eyes the same way. "Fin-sen," she said.

Celeste smiled and nodded. Was anything more moving than a young face on the verge of new understanding? She smoothed Najima's blankets and, without even thinking about it, leaned over to kiss her forehead.

"Good night," she said softly.

"*Layla sa'eedah*," Najima replied.

Celeste couldn't resist. She cocked her head. "What mins?"

Najima caught the joke, tossing it back with a grin: "Good night," she said in almost perfect English.

CHAPTER FIVE

Despite Elaine's grim prediction, Celeste approached the charge desk without fear. Over the past ten years, she'd learned to take in stride the ordinary Briton's distaste for Americans. She was smartly dressed, she lived in a good neighborhood, her ex-husband was an important man now married to a supermodel who knew even more important people. She was the very embodiment of that most cherished British ideal: respectability.

So why did the paunchy red-headed sergeant stare rudely when she described a case of what was clearly human trafficking? Why did he call over some of his fellow uniforms and say: "Go on, then. Tell it again," as if it were a joke?

Celeste told it again: the Farouqis' new house, the gala, her ex-husband and his partners, Begum beating Najima, Najima's escape, Najima's history. She told them what Flora had said about the kafala system and what she had learned online. Then she stepped back and did some staring of her own.

"Slaves," the sergeant said flatly.

"Yes, right here under your noses."

His fuzzy eyebrows shot up and Celeste realized that her choice of words implied the police were somehow derelict in duty.

"Slaves," he said again. "Sheiks."

"Only one sheik, actually." Was he really being sarcastic?

"Smuggled in from Jadal on private jets."

"Yes, the girls were drugged."

"Girls?"

"There are three more trapped in that house. We've got to get them out."

"Sounds like summat you'd see on telly," one of the constables remarked.

"It's not a show—it's real." Then she deliberately repeated: "Right under your noses."

"Mrs...." The sergeant glanced down at the scant notes he'd taken. "Stoneman. Are you under a doctor's care, perchance?"

"What? No!"

"Do you ..." He tipped up an imaginary bottle. "Maybe a little nip with the morning coffee, eh? Go on, you can tell me."

"I'd like to speak to your superior."

"What, me wife?" he said blandly, and the constables guffawed. Then the sergeant leaned over the high desk and Celeste took another step back. "Mrs. Stoneman, we don't look kindly on filing false police reports. You could get in a lot of trouble. You could be arrested yourself."

For once Celeste found herself speechless.

"Now then, others are waiting. Shall I have the constable walk you out?"

For the first time she noticed the line behind her.

"I can manage," she said in her frostiest tone. "But I'll be back."

As soon as the American woman was through the doors, the men burst into muffled laughter.

"I'll be baaahk," one said in very bad Arnold Schwarzenegger.

"Well, lads," said the sergeant. "That concludes our entertainment for the morning." He balled up his notes, squeezing them in his fist. "But if she turns up again, I want to be notified. At once. No matter where I am. Got it?"

The constables nodded, swallowing their questions.

The sergeant tossed the paper ball at the trashcan. It missed. He pretended not to notice. He called: "Next!"

◆ ◆ ◆

Although Najima continued to demonstrate great enthusiasm for Mrs. Flora's cooking, Mr. Benny (Mrs. Flora had explained that "Mrs." only applied to women, which horrified Najima: in Jadal referring to a man as a woman was a deadly insult, but apparently Mr. Benny just thought it was funny) seemed determined to introduce her to British delicacies: first fish and chips, then blood pudding, then kidney pie. The baby, however, objected. Vehemently. After those episodes, Mr. Benny stuck to ice cream—a different flavor every night. So far, the baby still kicked hardest for strawberry.

At first Najima thought the kicks were gas or indigestion, her body getting used to its improved diet. But then, in front of everyone, her blouse jumped all by itself—as if a little fist had punched it from within. Myrtle the midwife said it was a good sign: the baby was active. And everybody liked to watch for it. Najima let Mrs. Celeste and Mrs. Flora lay a hand on her belly so they could feel the kick, and both got dreamy smiles on their faces. Najima giggled, something she hadn't done for a long time.

Mrs. Celeste bought a framed print of the magic picture Starry Night and hung it on the wall opposite Najima's bed. Najima never tired of looking at it. The more you looked, the more you found to see. Did Fin-sen actually see the world this way? Or was he saying something about how everyone else sees the world? Perhaps what he saw was real and what everyone else saw was illusion. This perverse thought pleased her, though she couldn't say why. It was not an idea you could expect to see in The Judgments, where the world was one way only. One sky. One moon.

Mrs. Celeste joined her sometimes, bringing tea. Najima was learning English continuously—everyone was her teacher—but Mrs. Celeste also tried to learn the Arabic equivalent for every new word Najima picked up. They sipped their tea and consulted their dictionaries, using the magic picture as a primer.

"Moon," Mrs. Celeste would say, pointing to it.

"*Alqamar,*" Najima replied, and they both practiced.

"Tree," said Mrs. Celeste, pointing.

"*Shajara.*"

"Star."

Najima looked away, suddenly shy. "*Najima,*" she said.

Mrs. Celeste was startled. "*Najima?*" she said, pointing to the star. Then she touched Najima's hand. "Najima? Your name means star?"

She nodded. "Najima me." She pointed at the print. "*Najima* star."

Mrs. Celeste grinned and tapped her own chest. "Aljana," she said. "Celeste."

Now Najima was startled. Mrs. Celeste's name meant "heaven"? And where did stars belong if not in heaven? Was this a bizarre coincidence or divine intervention? She remembered what Mrs. Celeste liked to say—Flora had translated it for her: *kl shaksh yjb'an tuqarir linafsiha.* Everyone has to work it out for herself.

The second time Celeste attempted the police she took Flora. Flora had seen Najima's condition, had understood what the Farouqis said and witnessed how they treated the girls. Celeste hoped a different man would be on duty—she'd come yesterday in the morning; now it was afternoon; surely those were different shifts?

Her heart leaped when she did see an older man—silver hair, glasses—behind the desk. She introduced Flora and began their story again, but they were interrupted by the breathless appearance of the ruddy-faced sergeant. He halted by the desk, panting. He must have come running.

"Phil, step out for a smoke," he told the older man. "I'll sort things here."

Phil just nodded, stepping away. They watched him go. He seemed totally incurious. How could you be a good policeman without curiosity? Or was he, like the younger constables, cowed by the redhead's bombast and bluster?

The latter took his time settling in behind the desk. "Mrs. Stoneman," he said at last. Celeste was surprised he remembered her name. "Might I ask where in America you come from?"

Celeste tried not to roll her eyes. "Texas, originally."

Now he would ask if she could rope a steer or bust a bronco. They always did; they thought it was hilarious. But the sergeant glanced at his cronies as if confirming a bet. "And what is it you expect the Met to do?"

"I want you to investigate."

"Well, madam, I don't know how they do things in Texas, but here we don't investigate a crime without evidence of a crime."

The other constables snickered behind their mugs.

"There are lives at stake here!" Celeste snapped.

She described the threat Najima's unborn child—and any male child of Mehraj—faced from Tariq. She reminded him that the Farouqis had a private jet and could disappear at any moment.

The sergeant leaned over his desk. "Mrs. Stoneman," he said. "Ma'am." Did he actually drawl the word? "I could send every copper in this shop to knock on the door and inquire if there are slaves on the premises, but I think that would be a waste of everyone's time, don't you?"

"You could talk to Najima," said Flora.

"Why don't you bring her in so she can speak for herself?"

Celeste gritted her teeth. "It's dangerous for her to go out in public. They might have men watching."

The sergeant tapped his pen. "It wouldn't be a matter of proper papers, by any chance?"

"Of course, she doesn't have papers! She was smuggled in like contraband."

"Awfully convenient, wouldn't you say?"

The tapping pen was driving Celeste crazy. "I want to file an official report."

"Official, is it?"

"Yes, and I want to speak to your lieutenant. No, your captain. Commander. Whoever the boss is."

The pen finally paused. "I shall convey your wishes. And Constable Curry here will take down your statement."

One of the uniformed men stepped forward. "This way, please."

He led them into the squad room, a warren of bulky computers, overflowing wastebaskets, dirty mugs, and desktops buried under paper. Phones rang constantly. The young man offered the ladies tea, but, glancing at the mugs, they declined in unison. Celeste recited all the details once more. The constable was perfectly polite, but—unless she imagined it—there seemed to be a hint of mockery in his smile. When he finished filling out the paperwork, he stood up. This was as far as they were going to get today.

"Yee-haw," she heard one of the men murmur as she passed. Out of the corner of her eye she saw another tip an imaginary Stetson and point his finger like a gun. Yes, all Americans were cowboys. Constable Curry handed the sergeant the complaint forms. Celeste gave him a stiff nod and took Flora's arm. As they stalked toward the door, she heard the soft tinny sound of a paper ball hitting the trash can. This time, it seemed, he'd scored.

Celeste waited two more days. Then she, Flora, Abby, and Elaine piled into a taxi—Benny and one of his mates were home guarding Najima—and marched back into the police station. As Celeste had hoped, a different man stood at the duty desk-skinny, short, and dark—but they barely said "Good morning" before the paunchy redhead appeared, out of breath. Again, he nudged the other sergeant aside and took his place. Celeste realized someone must be notifying him that she was here. But why?

"Well, well," said the sergeant. "If it isn't Charlie's Angels."

Other constables, loitering near the desk with mugs in their hands, laughed. Nevertheless, Celeste told the story again, with Flora, Abby, and Elaine jumping in to add details.

"It's a powder-keg situation," Celeste finished. "The girls are in real danger."

"Powder-keg," the sergeant repeated, deadpan.

"What happened to the complaint I filed?"

The sergeant shuffled papers. "In process, madam. More important cases take precedence."

More important! Celeste stiffened her shoulders, and the other women did the same. "Then I demand to speak with your supervisor."

The sergeant's eyebrows shot up. "Demand, is it?"

Now all the women spoke at once, their voices rising to a clamor. The sergeant raised his own voice, and the lingering constables gave each other uneasy looks. Celeste kept the noise going until a tall man in a suit stepped out of the elevator.

"Sergeant Barnett," he said in a tone sharp enough to cut through the clamor. "What's all this fuss?"

Sergeant Barnett. She wouldn't forget that name.

The other man looked sheepish. "Some American ladies, sir, wishing to make a complaint. About slavery."

"Human trafficking," Celeste said hastily. "And probably a lot of money laundering too." Perhaps the mention of money would get this new man's attention.

"Ladies, this is Detective Chief Inspector Keene," Barnett put in. "Sir, this is Mrs. Celeste Stoneman and—" He hesitated but could not resist: "And her posse."

The inspector took in their faces, as well as the faces of the remaining officers. "Constables," he said mildly, "don't you have your assignments?"

Without a word the men put down their mugs, jammed on their caps, and scattered. Sergeant Barnett bawled after them: "You lot! Put those vests on!"

Detective Chief Inspector Keene paid him no more attention.

"Apologies on behalf of the Met," he told the women.

Celeste smiled. "In Texas we'd call that more heat than light."

He paused, studying her face, then said: "Please follow me," and led the way back to the elevator. No one said a word as they crowded together—it was, of course, illegal to speak in a British elevator. They followed Keene to his office, which was spare and institutional: immaculate desk, papers stacked on tiered trays, walls lined with filing cabinets and shelves, empty wastebasket. He sent for extra chairs, then offered everyone tea. This time they accepted. When at last all were seated with mugs in their hands, Keene looked at Celeste and said merely: "Please."

Celeste and Flora told the story once again, taking turns, Flora reporting what she had heard the Farouqis say in Arabic and what Najima had told her. DCI Keene took real notes. Celeste did too—from now on she was going to document every encounter with the police.

He wrote for a while, then looked up. "And where is this Najima at present?"

Celeste shifted uncomfortably. "She is…in seclusion. It's not safe for her to go out in public."

He gazed at them for a long moment, saying nothing. It was impossible to tell what he was thinking.

"Well," he said when no one else spoke. "We can send someone out to interview the Farouqis. Without making any unfounded claims, of course."

"That will just alert them," Celeste said quickly. "They'll run —they have a private jet."

He ignored this. "And we'll need to interview Najima as well." He glanced at Flora. "With our own translator. I'm sure you understand."

Celeste objected. "We can't…how do we know you won't simply arrest her as an illegal alien? She has no papers—she was smuggled into the country."

"You don't know," the inspector said evenly. "I couldn't possibly guarantee such a thing. But I can assure you that our primary interest is the human trafficking claim."

That was not much comfort, but Celeste saw they would get no further today. When she stood up, so did everyone else. The inspector shook their hands. He had pale eyes—blue or gray—and a tidy gray mustache.

"Can you at least keep watch on the Farouqi house?" she asked. "So you'll know if they run?"

"We hardly have the manpower for around-the-clock surveillance," he replied mildly. "Not based on this kind of evidence. But we'll be in touch. Thank you for coming in."

At least this time when they left the station house, no one was laughing.

Fadeelah struggled with two gigantic teddy bears, each more than half her size. A courier had shoved them in her arms—no doubt from a supplicant of the sheik's, trying to curry favor by sending extravagant gifts to his daughters. The stiff pink bows scratched her neck as she tottered up the back stairs. The sheik was entertaining business associates in the men's reception room—he'd invited them to see his new house, so soon they would be coming upstairs. She had to get these ridiculous bears out of sight.

The stairs exhausted her. As she trudged down the hall to the nursery, she heard Mr. Tariq's voice. She hadn't known he was in the house—he slipped in and out like a shadow. She paused for breath outside the office door. It wasn't quite closed, and she could hear Mr. Tariq's voice rising. He was either angry or excited. She hoped it wasn't angry—she often got walloped when it was angry.

He kept talking about Sarin, Sarin, whoever that was. A new maid, perhaps? Mr. Tariq's voice rose higher. Excited, not angry.

Then one of the bears started sliding out of her grasp. Fadeelah grabbed it but lost her balance and stumbled against the office door, bumping it open to bang against the wall. Mr. Tariq's voice cut off. In two strides he reached the doorway just as Fadeelah finally hauled both bears up, sliding her hands beneath the pink ribbons for better purchase.

When Mr. Tariq saw her, his face went stony still. There it was: anger.

"How much did you hear?" he demanded.

"Nothing, sir," she murmured, ducking her head. She tried to step past him, but he blocked the way.

"Tell me what you heard," he ordered.

"Just about the new girl? Sarin? Arrangements to pick her up?"

Mr. Tariq's face got scarier. That had not been the right thing to say.

"I really didn't hear anything," she blurted and squeezed past him. The bears interfered with her balance again and she almost fell on them. But she recovered her footing and hurried on.

Mr. Tariq called: "Wait. Come back here."

Something in his voice made Fadeelah break into a run instead. This was very foolish—there was nowhere to run to, the house was a prison, but pure instinct took over. Her body was telling her to flee, and her legs obeyed. Common sense told her she could never outrun Mr. Tariq, especially with this awkward burden, but her hands were stuck under the pink ribbons and her legs moved incredibly fast. She flew up the staircase to the third floor, gasping. He was coming. Where could she go?

Mr. Tariq bounded up the stairs two at a time. Fadeelah gave a little shriek—she couldn't help it—and dashed blindly down the hall into one of the guest rooms. Frantically, she freed one hand and yanked the French doors open just as he appeared. What now? There was nowhere to go! She had been foolish to trap herself this way.

"Now Fadeelah," Mr. Tariq said, approaching slowly. She was faintly surprised that he knew her name—usually he just called the maids "Girl." But his voice was wrong, and though he was smiling, his face was wrong too, his gaze as cold and steady as a cobra's.

"Now Fadeelah," he said again, "I don't know what you think

you heard, but you were eavesdropping, which is a very bad thing to do."

Slowly Fadeelah backed away, though there was nowhere to go but the balcony. She pressed herself against the railing. He was approaching. What could she do? She freed her other hand from the ribbon and tried to heave the bear at him, but all it did was drop to the floor.

"Please, sir." She froze in place. "I didn't hear anything. I won't tell anyone."

Now he let her see his fury. "So, you did hear—you know there's something to tell!"

He rushed her. Fadeelah clutched the remaining bear like a shield. The railing cut into her back. Then she felt Mr. Tariq's arms under her legs, scooping her up. "No!" she cried, but he swung around and opened his arms. She only had a moment to be terrified, but her wail escaped her like a long curling ribbon.

Tariq cursed, clutching the railing, looking down at the turquoise and gold tiles defiled with this *sharmoota's* body. Before he could think what to do, the courtyard was full of men in suits—his father's guests. They had heard, they had seen. There was no way he could secretly dispose of the body. Several men had their phones out, dialing 999. A chilling thought struck him: what if she wasn't dead? What if she woke up and talked? The entire house of cards he'd so painstakingly constructed would collapse—all his clients would pull out. For them, security breached one time was one time too many. His reputation would suffer even though he'd created a magnificent new marketing opportunity, an impeccable scheme. But if the girl talked, if the police came sniffing around, no one would touch it. And if he was exposed, Muhktar would certainly find out about the pipe deal. This girl, this ignorant piece of trash, could ruin all his plans.

Then he recovered his senses. He was a Farouqi; no one was

out of his reach, least of all a scrawny serving girl. People entered hospital all the time and never came out. He could arrange it. One way or the other, this Fadeelah would not speak. She would not spoil his plans or his profits. Meanwhile, he hurried down to join the men below and squat beside her, shaking his head, murmuring his concern to whoever might be listening.

Benny followed the ambulance to A&E and watched the attendants wheel the girl inside. His heart was still thumping —he could scarcely believe what he'd heard. He hadn't been far off when his mate called him. Reg had seen everything: a girl tumbling through empty air, clutching a huge stuffed bear. The man behind her, leaning over to watch. Luckily, the bear cushioned her fall, protected her head. Her left arm and leg took a great whacking, though. And if it was an accident, said Reg, he'd eat his hat. No one fell that way. That girl was dropped.

Shaky, Benny fumbled with his mobile and managed to get Mrs. C on the line. She gasped when he told her what had happened, then said she had to think.

After a long moment, she said: "Stay there, Benny. Find out what you can. I'll call you back."

Relief steadied him. "We've got a plan, then?"

"Oh yes," said Mrs. Celeste. "In about five minutes."

It actually took fifteen. If Benny's friend was right, if Fadeelah had been dropped, she was in even more danger than Najima —an attempt on her life had already been made. What could have provoked it? Tariq wouldn't kill her for sport—she must have heard or seen something he didn't want exposed. Which meant he would be anxious to shut her up as soon as possible. Therefore, it was crucial that they get to Fadeelah first. But how could they get her out of the hospital?

Celeste stared out the window, seeing not the street, the traffic, the weather, but hospital corridors, gurneys, medical personnel. A&E—Accidents and Emergency—was the British version of ER. Like their "ER": Thursday nights, George Clooney, big busy city hospital.

And with that, she had it. A smile spread across her face. The idea was bold, but it could work. It could. She would start by calling Willow into action—Willow's cooperation was vital. She would send Flora out for surgical masks and a large piece of black cloth. She would ring Myrtle and check in with Benny. She would brief her team. And then it would be game on, full-court press.

Still smiling, she went to tell the others.

CHAPTER SIX

The plan was simple: snatch Fadeelah. Right under the noses of the hospital staff and the sheik's security force, they would spirit her out and sprint to safety. They would set her up at home in the hospital bed Celeste would rent, with Myrtle the midwife popping in to check on her. But in order to pull this stunt off, Celeste told the others, they would need a distraction. A big one. So, she got out her phone and called the biggest distraction she knew: not royalty, but next best.

Willow, whose real name was Willa, had been dubbed *The Willow* while she was still modeling because she could bend her long supple body into almost any pose. She had kept the nickname when she quit the business and bestowed it on her wildly successful cosmetics line. As the face of the company and a CEO with a two-year-old son, she was always busy, yet somehow found time for her husband's ex-wife. In fact, they got on so well they were practically friends.

Willow's face and body had appeared in advertisements and magazines all over the world. Everybody recognized her, and unlike many celebrities, she had a good relationship with the press. If she called them, they would come. First Celeste told her the whole story, gratified to hear her gasp in all the right places. Then she proposed the distraction: Willow would hold a surprise press conference at the hospital.

"Support for breast cancer, maybe?" she suggested. "Or free cosmetics for women's shelters?"

"I can do you one better," Willow replied. "The girls and I

—" meaning Willow's top executives— "have been thinking of making a sizable donation. We hadn't yet chosen a charity, but I've just decided: we will donate a new wing to Free Trust Hospital. For facial reconstruction. That seems appropriate, don't you think?"

Now it was Celeste's turn to gasp. "A whole wing! Can you afford it?"

"Darling, we have to get rid of some money before the government takes it all. So, will a press conference outside the hospital do the trick? The crowd should provide you with camouflage."

"And you can arrange it all by tomorrow?"

"Darling, have you forgotten I sit on the hospital board? Now go plan your heist. I'll take care of the rest."

As soon as Willow rang off, Benny checked in. He'd been resourceful: the hospital refused to give him information because he wasn't family, but he had a mate whose wife worked there as a nurse. She found out that the young woman registered as Dee Jones had been treated in the Casualty Department for a fractured leg and shoulder. There didn't seem to be any internal bleeding. She had been taken up to the orthopedics ward for observation and was resting comfortably.

Celeste told Benny her plans and his part in them. In the meantime, he would watch the hospital entrance to see who went in and out. If he spotted anyone from *Hadiqa House*, he would ring Celeste at once.

"No worries, Mrs. C.," he told her. "Won't none of 'em get past me."

She was alarmed. "Benny, you're there to observe. Do not engage. Do you hear me?"

He promised, but there was a note in his voice that worried Celeste. Flora would chop her into little pieces if anything happened to Benny. But Celeste let him go. You had to trust your team.

The next morning, after the hospital bed and wheelchair were delivered, the women clustered upstairs before Celeste's full-length mirror. Najima, impeded by her growing belly, crouched awkwardly on the floor, draping the large square of black cloth so it covered Flora's ankles. Only Flora's face showed, as if the cloth had swallowed her whole. Najima showed her how to grab the fabric and pinch it closed at her throat. Flora hobbled about the room like an old woman, making everyone laugh. She practiced yelling in Arabic, Najima feeding her phrases. Flora bent her neck, hunched her shoulders, somehow turned her hands into claws. Her voice put on its own disguise: broken but shrill. She also turned out to be a pro at fake tears.

Then everyone wanted to try on the makeshift burka, pulling the cloth up till only their eyes showed. Elaine grumbled that it was hard to breathe. Abby kept tripping on the hem. Even Celeste took a turn, surprised at how stale the air tasted filtered through cloth. How could women possibly eat in one of these things? How did they breathe? Their movement and vision were certainly hampered. It was a pointed reminder of freedom she'd always taken for granted.

"Our turn!" Abby declared, handing out the Thursday Night scrubs.

As the rest of them got dressed, they practiced the Arabic phrase Flora had taught them: *Haya bina ya, Fadeelah.* Let's go, Fadeelah, come with us. Because of course the poor girl would be frightened: they were all strangers, no one but Flora spoke her language, and Flora would be off performing her own charade. Najima obviously could not come along on the mission. So, Fadeelah would be alone for a while without any idea who they were and where they were taking her. These girls had been through so much and it wasn't over yet.

Myrtle arrived to stay with Najima. Willow rang to say that the news conference was set and now she was getting dressed. Benny, who had kept watch at the hospital all night, checked in to say that the sheik had left guards at Fadeelah's door, and so many reporters were gathering outside with cameras and sound equipment it was hard to see who was who. One of Benny's mates had agreed to lend his delivery van to take Fadeelah home, and he too was on his way.

"Well then," Celeste said when they were all dressed. "I think we look pretty convincing." They looked no such thing, but she wanted everyone to feel confident.

The taxi was waiting outside. Celeste gave them all a last look, then drew them into a huddle. "Listen to me," she said. "We might be spoiled rich bitches with too much time on our hands, but we can do this. We have to do it—we're all that girl's got. So, remember, just because we're not heroes doesn't mean we can't do something heroic."

Everyone put a hand in and they flung up their arms with a whoop, startling Najima. Then they piled into the cab, promising the driver to double his tip if he could make it in twenty minutes. Celeste got to fulfill a lifelong ambition, saying: "Step on it!"

He made it there in fifteen, letting them out just as Willow arrived with her entourage. Willow's outfits were usually provocative—pink leopard print or something very brief with lots of zippers—but today she had chosen clothes even the Queen would approve of: a blue and green tartan coat dress, fitted exquisitely. She wore dark green over-the-knee boots, matching gloves, and a jaunty little hat. Willow knew how to dress for philanthropy.

Her assistants shielded her as she greeted reporters: "Hello, Rhys! Francesca, Simon! So glad you could make it! Nigel! Sandra, hello!" She apparently knew the names of every member of the press. No wonder they liked her so much. Dodging microphones and questions, she called: "Not yet, not yet! Wait till everyone's here."

That wouldn't be a problem: hospital employees in blue scrubs, white lab coats, and housekeeping uniforms were pouring out the hospital doors, along with administrators in business suits. More journalists joined the crowd, and curious passers-by stopped to watch.

As planned, Flora melted away. They would meet up with her on Fadeelah's floor. Celeste, Elaine, and Abby, just three more sets of blue scrubs, drifted through the crowd and into the hospital. Of course, they didn't have hospital ID badges, but no one at Registration paid any attention: they were too busy peering out the windows, asking what was going on. The women started climbing stairs, stopping at each floor to look for an abandoned gurney. Trolley in Brit-speak. They finally scored on lucky Floor Seven: an empty trolley parked against the wall. They took it by elevator—lift, damn it!—to the orthopedics ward.

Now for the tricky part. First, they located the lavatory where, as planned, Flora was hiding in a stall. She came out and they helped her drape the burka. No one had to speak. Celeste gave Flora's hand a squeeze, and they watched as she turned herself into a crone, hobbling down the hallway toward Fadeelah's room, clutching her burka under her chin.

Two members of the sheik's security team stood outside the door, impassive and impressively upright. The women watched from around the corner as Flora, ignoring the guards, went straight for the door. They blocked her. She said something in Arabic which, judging by the tone, meant: "Don't be ridiculous! Of course, I'm going in!" Then she launched into the tirade she and Najima had rehearsed, declaring that her daughter was inside, her only daughter, alone, afraid, in pain, needing her mother. When the guards kept shaking their heads no, Flora escalated, keening and wailing, throwing herself against first one man, then the other. They might have been stone walls and she a dried leaf for all the impact she had. But she was loud. The guards exchanged worried glances. The sheik had not mentioned mothers. But Flora was kicking up such a fuss that hospital security might come running and asking questions, which the sheik explicitly did not want.

Then Flora flung back her head and sucked in her breath. She was about to launch into ululation, the cry that Middle Eastern women made by clicking the backs of their tongues against their uvulas to express profound joy or sorrow. Celeste thought it sounded like the Indians' whooping war cry in old westerns. It was piercing. Shrill. People would notice. The sheik had told the guards to do their jobs quietly and discreetly. Ululating was neither.

Moving as one, each man lifted Flora by an elbow and carried her down the hall to the visitors' lounge. Celeste and her team did not wait. They pulled up their surgical masks and boldly pushed the trolley into the dim room lined with beds. They had only a few minutes.

"Here!" Elaine called.

They checked the chart hanging on the end of the bed to be sure. Dee Jones. A teenage girl with brown skin and long black hair was propped against the pillows, watching warily. Her left leg was in a cast, her left arm in a sling. They slid the trolley next to the bed on her right.

"Taking you for more x-rays, Miss," Celeste said loudly, in an execrable British accent, for the benefit of the other patients in the ward. They would be asked, so now they had an answer.

But Fadeelah shrank away. Celeste bent and pulled her surgical mask down so the girl could see her face.

"Fadeelah," she whispered. "Friend. *Sadiq*. Najima *sadiq*."

When the girl continued to stare, confused, Celeste put her hands over her heart and said "Najima" again. Then she repeated the memorized phrase: "*Haya bina ya, Fadeelah!*"

Fadeelah's huge brown eyes got even bigger. "Najima?" she whispered.

Celeste nodded vigorously, then put her arms together in the universal sign for infants, the rocking cradle. "*Tefl*," she added, remembering the word for baby. "Najima *tefl*." She patted her heart again as if to say she loved them both.

This seemed to do the trick. Fadeelah brightened and reached out. They helped her slide onto the gurney. She grimaced in pain but made no sound. Elaine ripped the blanket from the bed to cover her up. They could still hear Flora's wails, accusing the guards of stealing her daughter's honor.

"Her face," Celeste muttered, looking for something to

disguise it.

Elaine yanked the case off a pillow and wrapped it around Fadeelah's head, hiding her hair and obscuring her eyes. Then Abby took her own mask and looped it over the girl's ears. Ironically, all covered up, Fadeelah now looked like any respectable Jadali maiden.

"That's it," Celeste hissed. "Let's go!"

With two pushing the back and one guiding the front, they rolled the gurney out of the room and down the corridor in the opposite direction of the visitors' lounge, where Flora was lambasting the guards. Celeste guessed they had called hospital security to come take her but didn't know that most of hospital security was outside controlling the crowd or mooning over the star. Now Flora's voice was getting louder, which meant the guards were heading back to the room. Would they check inside? Celeste pounded the elevator button until the doors opened, and they rushed inside, hammering Close Door.

As the car dropped, Celeste bent over the figure lying tense on the gurney. *"Sadiq,"* she said reassuringly, touching her own chest, then the veiled head. *"Sadiq."*

The doors opened. Kitchen floor, just above the morgue. There was a dark joke in there somewhere, but this was no time for jokes: this was time to put the Primary Principle to work again.

"Act like you know what you're doing, and they won't pay attention," she instructed as they sped the trolley through the corridor and into a cavernous kitchen full of enormous steel appliances. Gigantic pots simmered away atop the stove, and two oven timers were going off. The kitchen smelled like boiled broccoli, but the few workers who hadn't rushed to the lobby were busy stirring and flipping and barely gave the group in blue scrubs a glance as they barreled past, heading for the service entrance. The van should be waiting; they were almost home free. Bursting through the doors, they rolled the gurney into the service parking area.

Which was empty.

"What's Plan B?" Elaine asked immediately.

There was none. But as she stood frozen, brain shorting out, Celeste heard mumbling and growling, getting louder. Then a battered delivery van careened around the corner in reverse, brakes screeching. Almost before it stopped, Benny burst out.

"Where's your friend?" Celeste asked as he flung open the van's back doors.

"Dodger got cold feet at the last minute," Benny replied in disgust. "But I hung onto the van, didn't I?"

Elaine and Abby hopped inside, where Benny had prepared a bed for the patient consisting of two sleeping bags covered by a tablecloth. Fadeelah cringed when he reached for her, but Celeste crooned: "*Sadiq*. Najima, Fadeelah. *Sadiq*."

Careful of her cast, Benny lifted Fadeelah, and handed her in to Abby and Elaine, who, careful of the sling, settled her on the makeshift bed. She had to be in pain, but she made no sound. Celeste scrambled in and slammed the doors while Benny got behind the wheel. With another screech, the van took off.

"What about Flora?" Abby yelled over the rumbling.

Did this truck have bad brakes *and* no muffler? What if they were stopped by the traffic police?

"Flora is very resourceful," she called back to Abby. "She'll find her own way home."

And indeed, after calling the two guards child-abductors, perverts, brutes, stinking goats, and diseased dogs, Flora managed to give them the slip. It happened when they returned to their post and opened the door to check on Fadeelah. When they saw the empty bed, they rushed in, forgetting about Flora, who took off, hurtling down the stairs, ripping off her burka, stuffing it into a trashcan, and disappearing into a crowd still enraptured by the combination of Willow plus cameras. Apparently, her company was pledging a shocking amount of money to finance a new hospital wing, specially dedicated to facial reconstruction. Oh, that was clever, even sly. Facial reconstruction from a purveyor of cosmetics.

Flora sifted herself through the crowd and onto the sidewalk. As usual, a line of taxis waited at the curb. She hopped into the first one and gave him the address. Maybe she'd even beat the others home.

Benny unfolded the rented wheelchair and helped ease Fadeelah into it. They took her in the back way in case anyone was watching. As soon as they shut the door, they were ambushed by a fifteen-year-old missile hurtling past to fling its arms around Fadeelah. Both girls burst into tears, then began jabbering in Arabic faster than Celeste thought people could talk. She was relieved when Flora walked in.

Fadeelah was clearly surprised that Flora spoke Arabic, and now the three of them chattered away with many looks and gestures toward Benny and the women. When the kettle whistled, they wheeled Fadeelah into the living room and helped her onto the bed, a tricky maneuver, since she refused to let go of Najima's hand.

Myrtle the midwife checked Fadeelah's cast and sling, gave her some paracetamol, and gently applied arnica to her new bruises. Everyone noted the old scars and scabs, so much like Najima's. Myrtle slid pillows under the broken leg and arm, took Fadeelah's vitals, and pronounced her fit enough, promising to look in again tomorrow.

Now, over hot mint tea and gingersnaps, Fadeelah recovered enough to sit up against her pillows and look at each of her saviors. A tumble of words poured from her mouth: Celeste only understood *shukran*—thank you—because Najima said it so often. When she paused, Flora asked the question on everyone's mind: how had she ended up smashed against the tiles in the Farouqi courtyard?

But Fadeelah ignored her, grabbing Najima's hand again.

"Jameela," she said urgently. "Dafiya."

No one needed a translation. Those were the other two girls still imprisoned in *Hadiqa House*. Najima and Fadeelah held Celeste's gaze, scarcely breathing.

Celeste laid her hand atop theirs. "First we need to know what happened to Fadeelah," she said through Flora. "Then, one way or another, we will get the others out."

She didn't actually say I promise, but the words hung in the air and, one way or another, everyone managed to read them.

CHAPTER SEVEN

It took Fadeelah three cups of tea to get through her story. She had to pause and start over while Benny fetched an extra chair and Celeste an extra teacup for their unexpected guest: Willow had managed to ditch her fans and entourage, hopped into her little Porsche, and driven herself to Celeste's house. She'd canceled all her appointments for the afternoon. She wanted to hear the whole story.

As did they all. Fadeelah started with the enormous teddy bears and ended with Mr. Tariq picking her up and dropping her over the balcony railing.

"Attempted murder," Celeste said. "Add it to the list."

"But I don't understand what made him so mad," said Abby, who was taking notes. "He chased her because she heard him talking on the phone? What was he talking about?"

"He was talking about someone named Sarin," Fadeelah replied after Flora translated. "I thought she must be the new maid."

"Sarin," Celeste repeated. "I don't think that's a person."

"Oi!" Benny cried. "That's what those knobs in Tokyo used, innit? The ones who tried to kill all those people on the Tube?"

Dear God, he was right. Celeste remembered: last March, the *Aum Shinriko*—some kind of homegrown terror cult, a mash-up of Hindu and Buddhist beliefs along with Christian apocalyptic prophecy. Their leader called himself Christ, Buddha, and Lamb of God. She hurried into her study to boot up the computer. They needed to know more. Why on earth would Tariq be interested in Sarin?

This time the Answer Box had answers. Celeste read the text out loud so everyone could hear. Sarin was a nerve gas, related to pesticides, that worked by paralyzing the muscles used for breathing, asphyxiating its victims. It could be mixed up easily in the most primitive lab, transported as a liquid, and activated simply by exposing the liquid to air, which turned it to poisonous vapor. The terrorists used plastic bags of Sarin which they dropped on the train and punctured with the sharpened tip of umbrellas, releasing the gas.

"Tariq is buying nerve gas?" said Elaine, incredulous.

"Maybe buying *and* selling," said Celeste. "And what better place than London? Everyone rides the Tube and everyone carries umbrellas—perfect camouflage." Then she caught her breath. "Flora, the umbrella in the vault!"

They had both seen it, but Celeste had taken a closer look: an ordinary black umbrella, every Englishman's appendage, with a stout handle and long shiny tip. But something had bothered her, something didn't look quite right, though she couldn't pin it down. Now she knew.

"The tip was too sharp," she said slowly. "That wasn't just an umbrella—it was a Sarin-delivery tool. A prototype, maybe."

"Tariq is a terrorist?" asked Abby.

"No. No, I don't think so." *I and myself against everyone else.* "I think he's doing business with them. Buying and selling Sarin, maybe other things. But I don't think he has a cause."

"Not like the I.R.A.," said Elaine, reminding them all of the recent London Docklands bombing.

Flora looked up, alarmed. "Do you think he's selling to the I.R.A.?"

"Maybe. I think he'd sell to anyone. I think above all else he's a businessman," Celeste replied. "And Sarin makes more sense than bombs: the chemicals are easy to acquire, it's easily made, with a foolproof delivery system. Easier to ship than bomb components, and a little goes a long way. I bet the profit margin is sweet."

"What mins?" Najima burst out. Flora had just finished translating the discussion, but Najima was looking at Celeste.

"If she means what do we do next, it's an excellent question," said Elaine.

Celeste shook her head. "We've got to go back to the police."

"But they laughed at us!" said Abby. "They refused to take us seriously."

"Maybe once they know about the Sarin?" Flora mused.

"We haven't got any hard evidence of that. It's still Fadeelah's word against Tariq's."

"But he tried to kill her," said Flora. "There's that."

"Again, her word. Tariq will say she lost her balance and fell."

Elaine scowled. "So, we go back and let the cops laugh at us again?"

For the first time since she was given a cup of tea and a cookie, Willow spoke up. Celeste had almost forgotten she was there.

"*I* have a suggestion," she said, her voice so compelling that everyone turned in their chairs, even the two girls who didn't understand what she said. "Let my assistant set it up. You and I will go together, Celeste, and we will be treated with respect." Then she smiled, showing the famous dimples. "I know *lots* of people."

The appointment was made. Willow drove them in her Porsche because she loved any opportunity to drive and had miraculous luck with parking spaces. Celeste could not understand how Willow folded her long body into such a tiny space. She herself struggled so much getting out of the car, she was afraid she might have to call for The Jaws of Life, which she wasn't even sure England *had*.

Their entrance—arm-in-arm—could not have been more different from the previous visits. Celeste worried about getting past the florid Sergeant Barnett, but this time, though he sneered, he uttered not a word. Celeste had time to wonder whether his problem was with women, with Americans, or just with *her* before she and Willow were engulfed by their welcoming committee. DCI Keene shook their hands and introduced his boss, the Detective Superintendent, his boss's boss, the Detective Chief Superintendent, and two men who, to judge by the cut of their suits and their Italian shoes, were civilians. Beyond them, the squad room was packed with police, everyone staring at Willow. Celeste thought they had probably been ordered not to cross the threshold. Also, not to speak, ask for autographs, or take pictures. Some of the men up front looked fairly bursting with the effort of holding back. Could staring too hard burn your eyes?

Willow gave her audience a merry wave and blew a kiss as DCI Keene led the group into the lift. As the doors closed, they heard the officers whistle and cheer. All but one, Celeste was sure. Sergeant Barnett glowered as they passed him.

They settled into Keene's office, joined by a stenographer, and Willow started talking. She told most of the story, turning to Celeste to fill in the blanks, ending with their suspicion that Tariq was dealing in Sarin. Celeste described the hospital stunt and explained why it was necessary.

"We believe this young woman would not have survived her hospital stay unless we got her out," she concluded.

The stenographer tapped nonstop on her little keyboard. Keene was taking his own notes.

"So," he said, looking up. "You are hiding two young women whose lives you believe are in danger?"

"Yes, and Najima is pregnant. Her child is at risk as well."

"Tell us again about the Sarin, if you would," said one of the civilians.

The men listened intently: none seemed inclined to dismiss these allegations as preposterous; no one mentioned hysteria or imagination. Celeste's shoulders relaxed a little. She repeated what Fadeelah had overheard and described the vault at Hadiqa House and the ordinary-looking umbrella with the very sharp tip. The men exchanged glances she could not read.

"Can you arrest him?" she asked. "Is that enough for a warrant?"

"We'll have to see about that," replied either the Detective Superintendent or the Detective Chief Superintendent—she couldn't remember which was which. "First we'll need to talk to the girls, using our own interpreter." He gave Celeste an apologetic smile. "No reflection on yours, of course. Just standard procedure. You can produce the girls?"

She answered reluctantly. "They're staying at my house."

Willow spoke up. "We're working on getting them emergency temporary visas."

Celeste glanced at her, impressed. This was the first she'd heard of *that*. No doubt Willow knew lots of people at the Home Office as well.

"Not to worry," said the boss. "We're not interested in their immigration status at the moment."

Celeste did not like "at the moment."

"We can't risk exposing them in public," she said, a bit sharper than she'd intended.

The boss nodded. "We'll come to you."

Celeste pushed further. "In an unmarked car?"

"I'm sure that can be arranged. Once we have the girls' statements, we can apply for a warrant."

"Apply? That could take days! Are you at least watching the Farouqi house?"

He gave her a professional smile. "The wheels only turn as fast as they turn, madam."

"Some wheels turn faster when they're greased," Willow remarked.

"Rest assured we have everything in hand, ladies," the boss replied smoothly. When he stood, so did everyone else. "Thank you for coming in. We'll be in touch."

DCI Keene escorted them back to the lobby. Celeste violated the unwritten law and spoke in the elevator. "*We'll be in touch?*" she repeated. "That doesn't sound very encouraging."

For the first time since they'd met, Keene smiled. His eyes

were the color of faded denim—how could she have ever thought they were gray? She wondered how he would look without the mustache.

"I am the senior investigating officer on this case," he said. "I give you my word we will waste no opportunity."

"And you'll keep us informed?"

He took out a business card and a pen, scribbled something on the back. "Here are my numbers at work and my personal mobile number. Call anytime, day or night." This time his smile was wry. "I never sleep anyway."

"Nobody sleeps," Celeste agreed.

"And try to be patient," he added, holding the lobby door for them.

"How patient is Tariq going to be?" she muttered as she passed. But she tucked the business card into her wallet, noting that Keene's first name was Charles. She wondered whether anyone ever called him Charlie.

The interpreter and another constable arrived at noon the next day, pulling their car around back as requested. Celeste wondered why there were two men. Did they expect to be overpowered by two traumatized teenage girls? She did not like the looks of either one. Nor did Flora, apparently, for she offered no tea, let alone a bit of lunch. The officers were young, white, and uncomfortable. Their eyes darted about the room as if looking for danger or contraband. But they did not ask to be alone with the girls—a relief since Celeste wanted to be sure they could trust the official translator's translation. She did not tell them that Flora spoke Arabic.

The girls seemed nervous while the police set up their equipment. Najima slid onto the hospital bed beside Fadeelah and held her hand. By the end of the hour, the interpreter had established that the Farouqis had held the girls against their will, abused and molested them—the translator colored every time he glanced at Najima's belly—until Celeste and her friends rescued them. At this point, Fadeelah looked over at Celeste and Flora to murmur yet again: "*Shukran, shukran,*" Najima chiming in.

The translator turned around to inform Flora and Celeste that *shukran* means *thank you*. They thanked him politely.

And the girls confirmed that the Farouqis were still holding two other minors captive, using them as slaves, and planning to acquire more. Flora gave Celeste a subtle nod, meaning that the translation had been accurate.

Finally, the constables packed up their equipment and said they would bring written statements for the girls to sign the next day. Celeste didn't know if Fadeelah could even write her name but said nothing. The two constables stood, awkwardly thanked Celeste, and took their hurried leave. Celeste still felt uneasy, even after they left. What was the matter? Was she the problem—getting paranoid, seeing enemies everywhere?

Flora now perched on the hospital bed with the girls, heads close together as they spoke rapidly. Celeste was dismayed to see tears shining in Najima's eyes.

"What is it?" she said, crowding onto the bed with them.

Najima said slowly: "They look us like disease." The fact that she used her rudimentary English to say this demonstrated just how wounded she was. She wanted to tell Celeste *herself*. Those were angry tears.

Flora, somehow fitting an arm around both girls, added: "She's quite right, you know. It's the brown skin. I get it too— hooligans calling me 'dirty Paki,' telling me to go home.'" She sniffed. "I've never even been to Pakistan."

"But these weren't hooligans," said Celeste. "These were police officers."

No one else seemed surprised. Flora nodded grimly.

"What is *wrong* with people?" Celeste exclaimed. But she might as well ask the walls or furniture.

To keep the girls' minds off their fears, Celeste bought an enormous stack of magazines, plus glue sticks and poster board. With Flora's help, she explained how to make a dream board: cut and paste pictures that show things you want to do, be, have. Pictures as metaphors for the intangible. It was good therapy, she thought, even a form of spiritual practice. At first the girls were dumbfounded. No one had ever asked them what they dreamed. No one cared what they wanted, what they hoped, what they preferred. Flora and Celeste had to demonstrate by starting a dream board of their own, grinning sheepishly when they saw they'd both chosen pictures of babies and baby products. Like Celeste, Flora and Benny had no children. Celeste and Flora had never discussed it, but from the start they'd formed a connection that felt utterly fundamental: despite their external differences, they always seemed to rhyme. And here was one reason why.

Once the girls understood, they attacked their own dream boards, chattering with excitement, paging through each magazine together, discussing the pros and cons of every picture, using Flora's sharp scissors to cut them out with surgical precision. Celeste and Flora exchanged another look, sharing the girls' delight.

Najima had already brought her pillow and blankets downstairs so Fadeelah wouldn't have to sleep alone in the big unfamiliar house. Likewise, Flora had brought an overnight bag from the garage apartment: she would sleep on the daybed in Celeste's study. If there were any problems during the night, she would be able to talk to both the girls and Celeste. She insisted she was there for the duration—Benny could look after himself, she told Celeste. They both knew he would show up for meals anyway. In his bachelor days, Benny had subsisted on beans and toast, but life with Flora had spoiled him. Now they all ate together, family-style, Fadeelah in her wheelchair. Flora, determined to put some flesh on the girls, also considered it her personal responsibility to nourish Najima's baby. Benny still brought home ice cream, which Najima was delighted to introduce to Fadeelah, whose eyes closed, at first bite, as if in prayer.

Tariq stationed four men outside, two in front and two in back, but entered the house alone. The alarm system presented no problem: he actually owned a security firm which used technology far more sophisticated than what the divorced *Amreekiyah* had chosen. He swiftly disarmed the system, used his best burglar tools to unlock the door, and stepped inside, silent as a snake, eyes already adjusted to the darkness.

He was gratified to see both little *sharmootas* together, the broken one in the hospital bed, the pregnant one curled up beside her on the floor. Two little birds, one little stone— or rather, one ceremonial dagger sharp enough to cut through bone. Which little bird first? He decided the broken one wasn't going anywhere, so he would start with the one who carried his father's parasite. A firm swipe across the throat ought to take care of both mother and child. Easing forward, the streetlamp outside providing the only light, he gripped the dagger.

Najima stirred. Something was wrong. Two years of scant sleep —summoned abruptly in the middle of the night or evading masculine hands that groped beneath her blankets—had sharpened her instincts. Even asleep, she'd known something was wrong. Fadeelah? Cautiously she slitted her eyes enough to see the peaceful figure lying on the bed. Not Fadeelah. But someone else was there, creeping forward, making no sound, yet she could practically feel his breath. And she could smell him. Citrus and bitter rosemary. That was Mr. Tariq's cologne. She had dusted the fine crystal bottle many times, sneaking a sniff now and then.

If Mr. Tariq was here, he'd come for the girls. She could call for help in English—Mrs. Celeste had taught her the words—but she did not do that. Eyes almost closed, she sensed him approach. Light from the streetlamp glinted off something gripped in his fist. This was definitely the moment to cry for help, but Najima did not. An instinct—a force—that had deserted her these last two years suddenly asserted itself: she came from a tribe of warriors. She would defend herself *and* Fadeelah. She was no longer powerless.

And she knew exactly what to do. The materials for the half-finished dream boards were still heaped by Fadeelah's bed. Timing had to be perfect. Najima stopped breathing. Waiting for him to get close enough was the hardest part. Within, the baby kicked. *Go to sleep*, she told it sternly. She hoped the blanket hadn't jumped.

Now. As Tariq raised the shiny thing, Najima rolled away, grabbed the scissors, then lunged at him in one heart-stopping move. Her belly unbalanced her, but she managed to plunge the blades into the meaty part of his thigh. She almost unmanned him. He cried out. The lights snapped on.

Najima struggled to her feet. Fadeelah sat up with a gasp, yanking the blanket to her chin. And Celeste stood on the stairs, holding up her phone. "I've already hit 99," she said, perfectly calm. "All I have to do is hit the last 9 and the police will be here in minutes."

Tariq's beautiful face scowled. Each time Celeste saw him, even now, she had the same thought: he was just a little smaller than you expected him to be. Muttering a curse, pressing on his wound, he gave Celeste a shrewd look.

"You don't want the police," he told her.

He was right, damn him. Ordinary local constables would answer the call, not the special case detectives. They would know nothing about Najima and Fadeelah: they would ask for papers, and when the girls could produce none, they would be hauled off to a detention center to await deportation.

"I don't want to," she acknowledged, "but I will anyway."

Before Tariq could respond, he suddenly collapsed, his feet swept out from under by a skilled swipe with a broomstick. Flora dropped the broom and pounced on his chest, one hand gripping a kitchen knife.

"Ah yes, the 'dear friend,'" Tariq said, recognizing her from the visit. He sighed, flicked her off him like a fly, and sat up.

"All I want is my property returned," he told Celeste, eyeing Najima's belly.

"Human beings are not property."

"Then call the police. What shall I tell them? Perhaps you've been stalking me, kidnapping my employees to lure me here. Or perhaps you are starting a brothel and these girls are the first in your stable. Perhaps you are…what is the word? When the old woman pursues the young man? Cougar. Yes, perhaps you are a cougar, and I am your prey. Which would be more humiliating when it appears in the papers tomorrow?"

"What is *wrong* with you?" Celeste cried, coming all the way down but staying out of reach. "What makes you think you can own another human being?"

"What makes you think I cannot?"

"I don't understand this me-against-the-world crap. You think you're superior to the *Bedu* you enslave. Americans think Brits have a stick up their ass. Brits think Americans are yahoos. East thinks West is corrupt. West thinks East is corrupt *and* barbaric. And on it goes, all of it used as a pretext for despising anyone who's not like you. *What is wrong with everyone?* We all bleed red!"

"I'm aware," Tariq replied, dabbing at the blood seeping through his trousers.

But before anything more could be said, they all whirled toward the sound of thumps and clatter and voices outside. It sounded like a struggle.

Tariq's phone buzzed. Shoving the dagger back in his belt, he answered. They could all hear the agitated voice, though they didn't all understand the words.

"Sir, we've got a big one out here, barely contained," the man was saying. "What do you want us to do with him?"

Flora understood the words perfectly. Shrieking, she hurled herself at Tariq, who seized her wrist and made her drop the knife.

"That's my husband," she cried in both English and Arabic. "Don't you touch him!"

Tariq let go and started backing toward the door. He gave Celeste an ironic little bow and said: "To be continued."

As he turned to leave, he deliberately knocked over the umbrella stand, kicking the scattered umbrellas so they slid across the floor. He met Celeste's eyes and grinned. Then he was gone.

A moment later, the door burst open, and Benny rushed in, disheveled, nose bloody, wielding his phone like a sword. Flora flew into his arms. "You all right, love?" he rasped, then looked at everyone else. "Anyone hurt?"

"We're fine, you great daft ninny," said Flora, dabbing at his nose with her nightgown sleeve. "What were you thinking, taking them all on like that?"

Celeste squeezed Benny's shoulder. "Thank God you were awake, Benny. Thank God you heard the text."

He gave her a sheepish smile. "I don't sleep so good without the missus."

"Now take off that shirt," Flora ordered, "and let me see to that blood before it sets."

Celeste made her rounds, checking each door and window, re-setting the alarm, though that evidently had not stopped Tariq. Tomorrow she would get a better system. Behind her, Benny was showing the girls how to high-five, teaching them a cheer. They were celebrating their victory. But Celeste knew there would be no more sleep for her tonight: coffee was what she needed. There was something marvelously normal, marvelously reassuring about the sound of coffee brewing. Yes, first she would call DCI Keene—he'd said any hour, day or night—then she'd go put the coffee on. Yes, that was what she would do.

And yet she lingered there, keeping watch at the window, gazing out at the empty street, worrying about how she was going to protect her family.

CHAPTER EIGHT

New alarm system. New locks. Motion-detectors. Floodlights. Everything but a moat full of sharks, and still Celeste felt uneasy. After two days of watching the street, migrating from window to window, she needed action. Something to do. How could they broaden their counter-surveillance? At last, she came up with a workable idea: Elaine's son, now at college in the States, had gone through a prolonged Goth period, painting his bedroom walls and ceiling black. Celeste remembered black sheets on his bed as well. Midnight black. Those would work. She called Abby and Elaine, who instantly agreed—they thought she didn't see how much fun they were having.

And sure enough, Elaine dug the black bedding out of storage, explaining a bit sheepishly that she hadn't had the heart to get rid of sheets her son had slept on. Celeste smiled for the first time all day. So, hard-shelled Elaine had a gooey spot after all. Girlfriends, sisters, co-conspirators—Celeste couldn't imagine life without them. She thought of the four girls in that horror house and all they had endured together. No doubt they felt the same about each other. Would the government separate them once the Farouqis were finally gone? Her smile vanished.

But then Abby and Elaine arrived with the sheets, and Celeste enlisted Benny in their mission. As expected, Benny responded with sizable enthusiasm and called some mates to come stay with Flora and the girls. Sexist it might be, he declared, but he was not leaving the females unprotected. One of his mates, a dedicated huntsman, brought along his crossbow. No one objected.

Celeste wrapped Abby and Elaine in the black sheets while the girls watched, giggling. With Najima's guidance, she made sure everything but the eyes were covered, then stepped back to judge the results.

"What about the sling?" Abby asked. "They'll look for a sling."

"I'll put their *ass* in a sling, and they can look for *that*," Celeste growled, making everyone laugh, though the translation eluded even Flora. "Anyway, we won't let them get close enough to see."

When they were ready, Benny carried Abby to the car. Because of course the real Fadeelah had a broken leg and Tariq's men might be watching. They took off, Benny driving at a speed just slow enough to let any observers spot Celeste and two huddled figures robed in black, but fast enough so they couldn't get a good look. As instructed, Abby and Elaine kept their heads down, while Benny and Celeste watched for any vehicle that might be tailing them. Celeste didn't expect to see a candy-apple red Lamborghini—not even Tariq was that reckless—but she thought she might recognize Jadali henchmen. In fact, she hoped to draw them out: she'd brought her notebook along to write down suspicious plate numbers.

But if someone was tailing them, he was doing a damn good job. After an hour of cruising neighborhood streets as well as commercial sections, Celeste started to worry. Worry *more*. Of course they were being watched, and if Tariq's men weren't tracking them on the road, then he must be using men on foot. In the park near her house, for instance, with its convenient stand of trees. As Benny adjusted the rear-view mirror, Celeste caught a glimpse of her face. She was scowling. Willow would say scowls created scary frown lines. Celeste hoped so. She wanted to scare the hell out of those thugs.

Abby, who was supposed to be keeping her head down, said "Look!" as they passed the botanical gardens. "An orchid show! We ought to take the girls. Fadeelah's nuts about flowers."

Celeste remembered the last time they'd been to the gardens, the day after the gala. She remembered thinking even then how much she would love to bring Najima there. And Fadeelah could come in her wheelchair. When it was safe. As they passed the YMCA, she said: "I bet none of them knows how to swim."

"I could teach them," said Elaine. She'd been swim team captain in college.

Abby pointed at a manicure parlor. "We could take them for mani's and pedi's."

"They'd be confused," said Elaine. "Not used to being served."

Abby went on dreamily. "And the Museum. The palace. St. Paul's."

"The zoo," said Celeste. "All those animals they've never seen."

"The Thames. The boats. The *ocean!*"

Celeste said: "Imagine just taking them shopping. Even Tesco would seem overwhelming."

"Harrods would give them conniptions!"

"How about taking them for Belgian chocolate crepes? Or to that place with the éclairs?"

Elaine raised her head, sneaking a peek as a cyclist rode by. "And teaching them to ride a bike."

Abby was awed. "That would be like giving them wings."

"Imagine," Celeste said, "teaching them to drive a car."

Everyone knew the significance of that. In Jadal, women were not permitted to drive or even sit in the front seat. If riding a bike gave them wings, driving a car would be giving them a Learjet: freedom, for the first time in their lives, to go wherever they chose. Except for Jadal. They could never go back. If they did, they would be executed, most likely by their own families. They would have to redefine *home*.

Then Elaine said flatly: "I think we're getting carried away. We're fantasizing."

"We'll sort it out later, "said Celeste. "Right now, we just have to think about getting the other girls out and keeping everyone safe."

But she knew Elaine was not wrong. Celeste was fantasizing months, if not years, to come. She was fantasizing a full house.

The girls needed asylum. Hell, they needed *passports*. She'd consulted the Answer Box: it was going to be complicated. Lots of acronyms. The girls would need an NTL, No Time Limit, stamp on the passports they didn't yet have. The NTL was necessary in order to secure the BRP, the Biometric Residence Permit, which, hopefully, would lead them to the ILR, Indefinite Leave to Remain. Celeste was hoping for the DL, Discretionary Leave, which could cut through red tape and accept refugees when compassionate circumstances applied. You'd have to have a brick for a heart if you didn't find these circumstances compassionate.

"What did you tell the boys?" she asked. "Will they help?"

"We told them the whole story," Abby said. "They promised to pull every string they can."

"Willow's doing the same," said Elaine. "That's a lot of strings."

"What did Neil say?" Abby asked.

"He'll help." Celeste grinned. "He doesn't have much choice, with both Willow and me harassing him."

She did not tell them the other thing Neil had said: that she talked as if the girls were her own teenage daughters. That was a little too close to fantasy.

The thought made her restless. Time to go home. Not that she didn't have faith in Benny's mates (and no one should ever underestimate Flora), but Celeste had been away from the girls long enough. She needed to see their faces. And remain vigilant. No doubt Tariq would choose his moment to attack.

"Benny, head home," Celeste said. "But keep your eyes open."

"I got 'em peeled, Missus," he replied. "I even sleep that way."

Benny steered with his right hand as he slipped the left into his pocket, briefly fitting his fingers ("big as sausages," Flora called them) through the holes of the jumbo-sized knuckle dusters. He was comforted by their weight. He'd spent several minutes in front of the mirror this morning, practicing his draw like a cowboy in a western. Was he fast enough for those goons? He hoped he'd get a second go. Meanwhile, he reminded himself to find a better hiding place for the dusters. If Flora found them, he was cooked. But those girls needed more protection than a broomstick or a kitchen knife. He grinned. They called him *Abi* Benny now: Papa Benny. He still brought home ice cream, hardly ever the same flavor twice, except for strawberry.

Flora finished making up the other guest bedroom—it was already spotless, but she thought fresh sheets would be nice. The two new girls would share the gigantic American bed. And when Fadeelah could climb the stairs, she could share with Najima. Imagine living with four teenage girls! Mrs. Celeste said she and Flora would be "house mothers," an Americanism Flora didn't quite get, but it sounded lovely. Of course, these weren't just *any* teenaged girls: their story was more complicated than most.

Besides—and this thought stopped her in her tracks—there would also soon be a baby. A *baby*. Mrs. C would have to buy a pram, a pushchair, plenty of nappies. The cot would go in Najima's room—there was lots of space—but perhaps they could keep the baby in a Moses basket when they were downstairs so the poor little tyke wouldn't be all alone. Giving the doorknob a bit of a polish—lots of germs on doorknobs—she floated down the stairs to the kitchen, where Fadeelah was waiting.

Each day was a continuous English lesson for Fadeelah and Najima, and everyone who entered the house became their teacher. What Fadeelah liked best, however, was to watch what Benny called "telly," particularly the cooking shows. She found it easier to learn when the speaker described what she was doing with her hands, so you could watch and listen at the same time. She especially liked the show called *Pastry Chef*. Serious cooks in white jackets and tall white hats created the most beautiful and elaborate cakes: some looked like gift-wrapped packages crowned with big bows, one like a big pink teapot surrounded by cups, one like an open treasure box spilling its jewels, but her absolute favorite was the cake heaped with brilliant flowers like a garden in Paradise. And *everything* was made out of butter and sugar: you could eat the teapot, the cups, the jewels, the flowers. Fadeelah was enthralled. Back home…no, Najima was right: it wasn't home anymore…back in Jadal, she'd helped her mother make all the pastries, all the sweets, demonstrating a natural gift. If she could learn enough English, and if the government let them stay, perhaps she could learn Western baking as well. Perhaps she could get a job in a bakery or restaurant, making beautiful cakes. Then she could teach the other girls—perhaps they could all work together. Even live together in their own little flat, though that seemed as plausible as escape had seemed only a week ago.

Meanwhile, the next best thing was to sit in her wheelchair watching Mrs. Flora cook. Since she made a lot of Middle Eastern dishes, much of the food was familiar, though Fadeelah rather liked the exotic British things with their odd names: Spotted Dick, which sounded like a disease but actually tasted quite nice; Toad in the Hole, which, Mrs. Flora promised, contained no actual toad; and Shepherd's Pie, made with neither goat nor sheep. What would the shepherds at home—that is, in Jadal— think about *that?*

Mrs. Flora talked as she cooked, explaining what she was doing, demonstrating technique, parking Fadeelah's chair at the table so she could chop vegetables and mix batter with her good hand. Mrs. Flora was using more and more English words in her explanations, and Fadeelah was learning. She was learning to be a free person. A voice in the back of her head seemed to continuously thank God for the angels who had rescued her. The front of her mind, though, was always preoccupied with whatever Mrs. Flora was doing in the kitchen.

Najima also liked learning by watching and often wandered into the kitchen to see what Mrs. Flora and Fadeelah were making. The wonderful aromas drew her, but she also had an ulterior motive: at the right moment, when no one was looking, she slid a small sharp knife out of its wooden block and stowed it in the pocket of what Mrs. Celeste called "sweatpants" and Mrs. Flora called "joggers." Two words for the same object. It was a lesson in itself. Which was the "right" term? And if they were *both* right, what did that mean about the absolute reality, the absolute truth, she had been taught as a child? Things no longer seemed so absolute. She thought of the poster on her wall upstairs, *Starry Night*, Fin-sen's vision of what was real, what was true. It made you call everything you knew into question.

But meanwhile, she carefully padded the little knife in her pocket with tissue squares taken from her own bathroom so Mrs. Celeste wouldn't notice any were missing. This was a justifiable crime: she would not be taken by surprise again. If it came down to that, she would not be taken at all.

A package-bomb might do the trick, but Tariq couldn't be sure the right people would get blown up. A boiler explosion, on the other hand, would very likely kill everyone in the house —an appealing notion. But how could he sneak someone in to tamper with the boiler? The whores were being especially cautious, that big lout was always hanging about, and Tariq suspected that an unmarked police car cruised past the house at unpredictable times. He thought wistfully of poisonous snakes —so much poetry in that idea—but again, how could you be sure they would bite the right people? The interfering *Amreekiyah* had made everything more difficult.

Then he remembered that last April, in Oklahoma U.S.A., a man named Timothy McVeigh had blown up a federal building, killing many, injuring hundreds more, destroying buildings within a sixteen-block radius. Overkill, perhaps, but undeniably efficient. McVeigh was an idiot, of course—caught ninety minutes after the explosion for driving without a license plate *after he'd just blown up a building*. Tariq couldn't help laughing. But he could still learn from McVeigh, who'd used ammonium nitrate fertilizer mixed with liquid nitromethane and a water-gel explosive. Not hard to come by. And more effective than dynamite: he'd read that the blast could be heard 89 kilometers away, that broken glass accounted for five per cent of the deaths, and that in some cases, limbs had to be amputated without anesthesia in order to free people trapped under the rubble.

Tariq's bomber could drive the loaded truck right up to the house. And if the man could not get away in time to save his own life? It would not be hard to convince him to sacrifice himself, not when the reward was eternal Paradise, where he would recline on a silk couch while seventy-two virgins fulfilled his every need. Virgins whose hymens grew back every night so they would always need deflowering.

Tariq grinned. Even his mother might be troubled by that grin. Then he reached for his mobile. Time to go shopping.

Flora paused, dust-rag in hand, to look at the girls' latest dream boards. Mrs. Celeste kept them supplied with glue sticks and all kinds of magazines: fashion, home and garden, electronics, art. They had each made three boards so far, propping them up on opposite sides of the room. Flora glanced up as Celeste joined her, new binoculars slung around her neck.

"Different sides," Flora pointed out. "Claiming their own territory."

Celeste nodded. "Declaring their own sovereignty. That's a good sign."

Fadeelah's boards were covered with pictures of flowers, cakes, baking supplies, young women hugging or striding arm-in-arm. And sweatpants—both girls had found pictures of sweatpants in catalogs to show their enthusiasm for the marvelous invention—as marvelous as ice cream—that kept them warm, comfortable, and modest. Mrs. Celeste had even found some for Najima with maternity panels.

Najima's boards were more complicated: pictures of babies and baby items, but also pictures of paintings that caught her eye. Celeste saw that she'd found another Van Gogh—the ecstatic sunflowers. A good balance with *Starry Night*. Najima had also cut out pictures of books, translating their titles to Arabic with Flora's help and scrawling them in red ink. She'd even pasted a picture of a computer, writing *The Answer Box* beneath it. When Flora translated, Celeste laughed out loud. It felt good. She had not done much laughing lately.

"They can't wait to show Jameela and Dafiyah how to make dream boards," Flora said.

"That's because no one ever taught these girls to dream."

"No one wants slaves who dream."

Celeste agreed. "That would be dangerous."

"Do you think we'll get them out? The other two?"

"Do you trust the cops?"

Flora's eyes met hers. "Some of them. I like Keene."

"Me too. But what I've learned so far tells me not to count on anyone else. We wouldn't have gotten this far if we hadn't acted ourselves."

"If *you* hadn't acted."

Celeste shook her head. "I couldn't have done anything alone. I couldn't have got Najima out of that house in the first place without Benny's help."

Flora's smile warmed. "Yes, he's become quite attached to the girls. And they to him."

"That's good for everyone. These girls have to learn that *some* adults can be trusted."

"What will become of them? Ultimately?"

Celeste shook her head again. This time it meant *I don't know*. "One step at a time, my friend," she said, squeezing Flora's arm. "The Chinese say that's how you complete a journey of a thousand miles. Take a step."

But she was having trouble following her own advice. The little masquerade this morning had accomplished nothing: they hadn't lured any spies out of the shadows or noticed anything suspicious. And now she was stuck going from window to window again, unable to hold still. Nothing seemed out of order on the street, though once, when a dark sedan passed the house, she thought she recognized Keene. But who could tell from this distance? The window in her study overlooked the small park, where people walked expensive little dogs who peed on well-established trees. Even in their current leafless state, the trees provided good cover. The park troubled Celeste. Anyone could hide in there.

"You're going to wear a path in the carpet," Flora grumbled as Celeste passed her yet again.

Najima patted the pocket of her bulging sweatpants. She was standing in front of the hall mirror, contemplating the globe of her stomach, checking on the knife. It was still safe, wrapped in its wad of toilet paper. She rather hoped Mr. Tariq would try again, because she would appreciate another opportunity to sink the blade into his flesh. Maybe next time her aim would be better. She grinned at the mirror. Who was this new bloodthirsty creature? Perhaps she had more in common with her big brother than she'd thought.

Then the grin vanished as she imagined Ghassan, the rifle he wore slung over his back now in his arms, pointed at her. All he would see was the belly. All he would feel was shame. All he would think was *she has dishonored our blood*. He would squeeze the trigger without hesitation. He would kill his sister and her child…for what? An idea? What was "honor" but an idea?

And why had the question never occurred to her before?

But what *she* thought didn't matter. Ghassan was the one with the gun and maybe young Abdullah too by now. And behind them stood a crowd of cousins and uncles and neighbors —nearly everyone in the tribe shared blood with everyone else —with their rifles raised too. Cocked and loaded. No, she could never go home.

She would never see her mother again. And Zainab would never meet her grandchild. The thought stuck like a hatchet in Najima's heart. But one thing she'd learned during captivity was to face facts. Never going home was a fact. Honor was just an idea. And she had a right to her own life. That was an idea too, but a better one. As for her child, her sinless child whose history was clean and blank—no one had the right to steal his life either.

She could still sense the girl she'd been—free, naïve, a bit wild —but there was something more now. It was as if the grown Najima had stepped in front of that girl to shield her.

Wandering back into the living room, she studied her dream boards. Pictures of pacifiers, teething rings, rattles. The baby was real. A fact. In just a few months he would enter the world, a separate person. A baby she would hold in her arms instead of lug about in her belly. The thought made her shiver. Plenty of Jadali girls became mothers at fifteen, but they weren't like her, alone and hiding in an alien culture like a criminal. Those girls still had their own mothers.

For just a moment she imagined Zainab cradling her new grandchild, crooning the same ancient lullabies she'd sung to baby Najima. She imagined joining her voice to Zainab's, continuing the song by herself. Tradition passing from mother to daughter to child. It would have been a sweet moment.

But—facts were facts—she would never get to experience that moment. She looked at the other pictures she'd glued to her dream board: books, computers, English words she wouldn't always have to translate into Arabic. Then wisdom spoke to her, an unfamiliar voice in her head. It said: singing with your mother to the baby *would* have been a sweet moment, but can you be happy without it? The answer was clear: despite the risks and uncertainty, despite all she'd been through, she could be happy. She would seal Zainab away in a pocket of her heart, open it only when she needed to weep. She could do it. She could let her mother go. There would be plenty of heart left over, and there were other kinds of happiness. It came in flavors, like Benny's ice cream. And her child would not grow up to be one of those warriors with a rifle slung over his back.

The expensive binoculars had proved to be worth every penny: Celeste spotted no Lamborghinis, but then she didn't expect to. Way too obvious. But she could watch the park from her study window: any movement, even a dog lifting its leg, was discernible. Like...*that*. A figure—a man in a tan overcoat—had just stepped behind a pine tree. She waited for him to step back out. She waited. What was he doing back there--urinating? Oh, not the Brits. At least not the Brits in this part of town. Perhaps he was watching *her.* Maybe it was *her* turn to spring a surprise.

Slinging the binoculars around her neck, grabbing her coat, her phone, and the scissors from the dream board pile, she yelled "I'm going out!" to no one in particular, dashed outside, then halted. How should she approach? Head on? That was her inclination—so American—but perhaps not the wisest move: what if he ran? An ambush, then. She would circle behind the houses and approach from the far side of the park. He wouldn't see her coming. And then? She punched 99 on her phone just in case, easing it back into her pocket. All it needed was one more 9. She kept hold of the scissors. Flora had cleaned the blood off and sharpened the blades. It wouldn't hurt to let him see.

Carefully, and much slower than she wanted, she approached the big pine tree from behind. Yes, there he was. Tan overcoat. Did Tariq's thugs wear tan coats? This man was tall enough but not a hulking muscleman. And even from behind she could see his hair was gray. Tariq's men were all younger. Holding the scissors out defensively and keeping one hand on her phone, on that last 9, she inched her way toward the lurking spy. He didn't look Jadali, even from behind. Could Tariq have hired local muscle? Did he have men planted throughout the neighborhood, awaiting his command? And what could she do if he did?

Then, as if sensing her, the man turned around.

"Detective Chief Inspector!" she said, astonished.

He glanced down at the scissors she was still pointing. "Are we fighting a duel? I'm afraid I left my rapier at home."

CHAPTER NINE

After they found an elderly yew with branches broad enough to hide them both, Keene cleared his throat and began: "Mrs. Stoneman—"

But Celeste interrupted. "Listen, I can't keep calling you Detective Chief Inspector—it feels like I'm on *Masterpiece Theatre*. Your first name is Charles, right?"

Keene's expression did not change, but he did something with his eyes that warmed his whole face. "Yes, though most people call me Keene."

"And I'm Celeste. I'd ask what on earth you're doing here, *Keene*, but it seems pretty obvious."

Now he looked dismayed. "*Was* I obvious?"

"Well, I do have these." She lifted her binoculars. "But aren't you too important to be surveilling us personally?"

He fiddled with a button on his overcoat. It looked loose. Why had no one sewed it on for him? "Things are beginning to happen. Things I can't talk about. Yet," he added hastily.

Frustrated, Celeste turned and gave the tree a kick. "Lord! I feel like a donkey caught in a Texas twister: can't run, can't hide, can't make it stop."

To her surprise, Keene laughed. "Yes, I've heard some mention of Texas."

"Well, after college, I did move to New York. I'm not a *cowboy*."

"I fear I must apologize for some of my fellows."

"Especially that boneheaded sergeant."

"Barnett?" The smile vanished. "What did he do?"

"He implied I was unstable — asked if I was under a doctor's care. Then he asked if I'd been drinking and accused me of filing a false police report. He egged his men on—used me to put on a show."

"I do apologize on behalf of the Met." He looked as if he was going to say more but stopped.

"Well, once you found us it didn't matter. It just burns my—ticks me off—to be called a liar. Flora and I had just come from that house of horrors, and we were still shaky."

"Tell me about the house again. Don't leave anything out, no matter how small."

Once again, she walked him through the visit: the wives, the antiquities and blades, the way Fadeelah and the other girls were treated, the missing documents she suspected Tariq stole, the cat-and-mouse game he played with her, the hidden elevator —she remembered to say "lift" just in time—the huge snake guarding the vault.

"Snakes," Keene mused. "An interesting touch. If I'm not mistaken, snakes in ancient literature represent fertility. Also, guardianship, I believe, and vengeance." Then, ears pinking, he added: "Funny, that. Something I must have picked up at uni long ago."

"Funny what things stick," Celeste agreed. "Apparently, I remember every word of the Texas State Anthem, which I learned in fourth grade. Would you like to hear?"

"Most certainly."

So, Celeste laid her hand over her heart and sang the first two lines:

Texas, our Texas! All hail the mighty State!
Texas, our Texas! So wonderful, so great!

Keene let out the biggest laugh yet. "*So wonderful, so great*? Really?"

"Yep. We grow poets like Kansas grows corn."

They grinned at each other. It took Keene another moment to say: "But I interrupted. Please go on. Tell me about the vault."

Celeste described everything she could remember, including the umbrella with its sharpened point. "Why do you think he let us see that?" she asked. "Wasn't it risky?"

Keene nodded. "But it fits his profile. Arrogant. Confident. Someone who enjoys playing God, manipulating people, controlling things. It makes him feel powerful."

"Oh, and when I asked him if business was good, he gave me a creepy smile and said: *Business is booming.*"

"That was the word he used?"

She nodded. "*Booming.* Now it sounds so sinister. You think he was toying with me?"

"I will certainly inquire once we have him cuffed and contained," he replied evenly, and Celeste understood that, despite his calm demeanor, Keene would make a dangerous foe. It cheered her immensely.

But as it seemed he was not going to reveal any more about the case, Celeste found herself asking about his own background. He told her he was widowed—his wife had died ten years ago after a long illness—and had a grown son, Geoffrey, an architect with a firm in Leeds. The firm designed huge business parks, but Geoffrey's secret ambition was to build a cathedral—he showed his father sketches whenever he came to visit.

Celeste was charmed. "And does he have a mustache too?"

"A mustache? No, why do you ask?"

"I thought maybe it was a family tradition. Young men sometimes grow one to make themselves look older." Keene frowned, but Celeste went on: "It sounds like you and your son are close."

"He's a good lad." She could hear the affection in his voice. "Rolls up his sleeves when he visits and helps me dig in the garden."

"You're a gardener?"

"My wife was. She won prizes for her dahlias—so many variations, each one a stunner. I try to keep it up."

"As a tribute."

"And a memorial. The garden is her final resting place."

Celeste was startled. "She's buried in your garden?"

"Well, her ashes, you know. Scattered with the fertilizer. That was her wish."

"And how do the dahlias feel about that?"

He smiled. "So far they seem quite enthusiastic."

"I've never had a garden but I'm thinking of putting one in this summer. The girls seem smitten with flowers, especially Fadeelah. I think they'd really enjoy growing their own." Then she added with a grimace: "If they're still here."

Keene tugged his loose button again. "Perhaps I could help?"

"With the flowers or their asylum?"

"Both, actually. I'll have a word with some chaps I know at the Home Office, and I would be happy to help with the garden: advising or digging or whatever you need." Then he added: "I could bring you some dahlia tubers."

Celeste blinked. Brits could be excruciatingly polite, but this offer went beyond professional duty or even common courtesy. Didn't it?

Cautiously, she replied: "I don't think there's room for a *big* garden."

"Oh, you can do wonders if you make use of vertical space." He counted off with his fingers: "You can build towers with pots that stack or hang in layers, trellises for the climbers, tiers with elevated beds, lattices, pyramids, obelisks, even repurposed ladders..."

Celeste grinned, picturing the Detective Chief Inspector in gardening gloves and a floppy hat. His ears were still rosy. Was it only the cold? A light rain had begun to fall. She tightened her coat, tucking her hands under her arms to warm them.

Keene stopped abruptly. "Do forgive me. I've been rattling on while you're freezing. Please, allow me to escort you home."

"I think you should stay incognito for now. And you weren't rattling on; the garden sounds *lovely*, and I hope we get to make it." Then, barely aware she was doing it, she laid her hand on his sleeve. "But you never did say why you're surveilling us personally."

He hesitated.

"Whatever it is, you can trust me. I'm not the whack job Sergeant Barnett thinks I am."

Keene's gaze met hers. "Mrs.—Celeste—I have never considered you a whack- job. I have never doubted you for a moment. I'm here myself because I'm not sure who else I can trust."

"Who else? Are you talking about the *police*?"

He shook his head, taking her arm and firmly turning her around. "I can't say more now. Please go home before you catch a chill."

"But you'll tell me eventually? When you can?"

"I have enjoyed our talk. Good afternoon, Celeste."

That was crystal clear. "Good afternoon…Charles."

Celeste didn't think a man as self-possessed as Keene ever said anything off-handed. There was more to this story than she knew. What was it Keene had said? *I've never doubted you for a moment.* She shivered, perhaps from the cold, tightened her coat, and hurried home.

The next time he came, he chose a bigger tree and wore a darker jacket. But Celeste spotted him with her binoculars, and—glad she'd sprung for the Deluxe Nikon Mountaineers with Super Mega Zoom—ran to get her coat. She was just slipping out the door when Flora called her back and handed her a thermos.

"Hot tea," she said firmly, as if refuting an argument.

Flora knew Keene was out there, that Celeste was going to meet him. But why should that be a surprise? Flora had always seemed to have her own built-in Super Mega Zoom.

"Will I ever be able to keep a secret from you?" Celeste asked her.

Flora smiled. She could give the Mona Lisa lessons. "Next time just bring him home."

Keene looked pleased to see her but said: "I'm not sure this is wise."

"Why don't we go back to the house? You can surveil us up close."

"I don't think that's the best way to protect you."

"We sure could have used you the night Tariq broke in."

He warmed his hands on the thermos. "Tell me about that again."

"Again?"

"Everything you remember."

As he sipped the steaming tea—Celeste thought next time she'd bring a handful of gingersnaps as well—she reconstructed the invasion, adding details Najima, Flora, and Benny had provided.

"If Najima wasn't such a tough little cookie, who knows what might have happened?" she finished.

"I think we do know."

"He would really have murdered two young girls? And the baby?"

"Greed and power make men commit the unthinkable."

"He's already rich!" Celeste kicked a pinecone. "He's already powerful!"

"I've learned that power is a leaky bucket—it can never be filled." He shrugged. "Aren't there always men who are richer? More powerful? There's always another rung to climb and always someone right behind you. Didn't you say you think he swindled his own father out of the pipe contract? Men like Tariq need to keep proving they're on top. I don't think the word *enough* is in their lexicon."

Agitated, Celeste stomped on another pinecone, trying to grind it underfoot. "It can't be he feels insecure. He thinks his nation, his *tribe,* is superior to everyone else. He thinks he's entitled to whatever he wants. He's like a comic book villain, only real."

"Fortunately, I don't have to understand him. All I have to do is catch him."

"But *I* want to understand." She picked up the pinecone and hurled it. "Tariq, the traffickers, the terrorists. I don't get it. This contempt for human life. This refusal to acknowledge the value, the *autonomy*, of every human soul. This stupid hate! I keep asking: what's *wrong* with people?"

Keene stepped forward to shield her from the sharpening wind. "I don't know, but it's been wrong for a very long time. Perhaps it's something we're born with."

"You think we enter the world with hate and greed already planted in our cells?"

"I think the *potential* for it is an ugly aspect of human nature."

"I wonder if animals hate."

"When I was a boy, our neighbor's bulldog tolerated everyone but me. The very sight of me drove him into a frenzy. He would lunge to the end of his chain, snapping his jaws, then growl as long as I was in sight. I have no idea what he held against me. I was just thankful we had a back door."

Celeste laughed. "Tell me more about this boy."

Keene finished the tea, handing the thermos back. "Only if you'll trade me bit for bit."

"That seems fair."

"Then it's your turn."

After trading lots of childhood details—parents and siblings and summers and school—Celeste decided she felt perfectly comfortable with DCI Keene, comfortable enough to tease him when he flat-out insisted there could never be a real band called Kinky Friedman and the Texas Jewboys.

"What?" she said. "The BBC didn't play *Ride 'Em, Jewboy*? That one's really about the Holocaust. Or *We Have the Right to Refuse Service to You*? He specialized in songs about outcasts. But my favorite is *They Ain't Makin' Jews Like Jesus Anymore*."

"Are you inventing this?"

"Not even a little. That one's a protest against racism."

Keene was shaking his head. "But the name of the band! I should think they'd be arrested."

"You've never been to Texas. And you've never been the only

Jewish girl in your eighth-grade class."

"No, I must confess that I have not. But are there really so few Jews in Texas?"

"No, but I grew up in a small town where the dominant religion was football."

He laughed. "That may be true here as well. But how did it affect you—being an only?"

"I got used to being *other*. Jews are scattered so far across the world that we're always *other*—the outsiders whose God and holidays and beliefs are different from everyone else's. That's one reason why I sympathize with Jadali refugees."

He began another question, but she stopped him. "Nope, your turn. It was your turn three bits ago."

So, they tossed the conversation back and forth, like a game of catch, endlessly comparing: *ER* vs. *EastEnders*, American Football vs. The Rest of The World's Football, divorce vs. widowhood, Elvis Presley vs. Henry Purcell, Rocky Road vs. Rum Raisin, Walmart vs. Tesco, private vs. public school (apparently in England, "public" *meant* "private," as if things weren't already confusing enough), whether sunshine was overrated, what *jumper, biscuit,* and *boot* really meant, and who actually dumped the tea in Boston Harbor. By this time, they were laughing, and Celeste almost forgot why they were there. Charles Keene, however, had not. He kept flicking glances over her shoulder to the streets beyond the trees. Even though he returned his sharp blue gaze to her face each time, she knew he was keeping watch.

Still, the game went on until they were interrupted by Keene's mobile. He dug it out of his coat pocket—not a sleek new Motorola like hers, but a bulkier model with an aerial—and turned away to talk. The call was brief. She barely had time to kick another pinecone before Keene stuffed the phone back in his pocket and said: "I'm afraid I must go."

"Is something wrong? Is it the case?" When he hesitated, she pressed: "You said you trust me."

"I do trust you."

"Well, you might inform your face."

He didn't smile, and for a moment she was afraid she'd gone too far—vulgar Americans always getting too personal—but then he put a hand on her arm and said: "There's a reason, besides general police stoicism, that I try to remain impassive. I'm breaking all kinds of rules to tell you this, but...we think we have a mole."

She knew he didn't mean a garden pest. "In the *Met*?"

He gave a grim nod. "We've narrowed the possibilities down and we're preparing a trap. But right now, I'm not completely certain which of my colleagues I can trust. That call let me know that the trap has been set."

"How can I help?"

He shook his head. "For now, I want you to go home and stay there. Don't expose yourself or the girls. Wait until you hear from me."

This stern and sober Keene was different from the polite diplomat or the relaxed new friend she'd been getting to know. This Keene revealed the field-hardened all-business professional. She had to admit it was a tiny bit thrilling. But mainly she was alarmed.

"What if a constable comes to the house? How will I know whether to let him in?"

He paused. "I'll give you a code word."

That was definitely thrilling. "I've always wanted a code word!"

Something in his gaze eased. "Shall we say...Boston Harbor?"

"Boston Harbor." She nodded, and he turned her around to face the street.

"Go home and stay there, Celeste, until you hear from me."

She started briskly toward the house but couldn't resist tossing back over her shoulder: "Look sharp, Watson! The game is afoot!"

Behind her she heard what might have been a dry little laugh, but when she looked, he was already gone.

CHAPTER TEN

She recognized his knock. That was impossible, of course, but she was certain just the same. Still, what was the point of having a password if you didn't use it? Waving Benny back, she unlocked the door and cracked it open.

"Who goes there?" she demanded.

"I think you know," came the dry reply.

Celeste made her voice gruff. "What's the password?"

She heard a sigh she was probably meant to hear and realized that he was playing too. "Boston Harbor."

She swung the door wide. "Enter, friend!"

Ignoring Benny's watchfulness and Flora's little smile, Celeste took Keene's coat and hung it up. He was holding a fistful of pink stargazer lilies.

"Those can't be from your garden," said Celeste.

"No, but they are from a shop called Green Gardens." With a slight bow he presented one lily to Celeste and another to Flora, saying "How do you do, Mrs. Butters? I remember you very well." Then he approached the two skinny girls peeking out from behind the corner. One was in a wheelchair and the other —obviously pregnant—stood over her, one hand clenched in her pocket. Keene knew who they were, but he waited to be formally introduced, then handed each girl a flower. He did not stare at Najima's severely cropped head.

Fadeelah broke into a huge smile, hiding her face in the pink speckled petals. Najima was a little more wary, but she too sniffed her lily.

"This is Benjamin Butters, Flora's husband," said Celeste, and the men shook hands.

"I'm afraid I have no lilies left for you, sir," Keene said with a straight face.

"I'd have summat to say if you did," Benny growled, but his smile was good-natured.

"Let me show you what the girls have been working on," Celeste said, taking Keene's arm to lead him into the living room.

"Is this a social call or is something happening?" she murmured once they were out of earshot.

"If we've got our ducks in a row, something should happen very soon."

"You can't say what?"

Keene only cocked his head to study Najima's dream boards. He asked what the Arabic meant, and Celeste called Flora over to translate. The others trailed after. Keene seemed genuinely interested in the images the girls had chosen.

"Fadeelah is indeed enamored of flowers," he said.

"Yes, I found her some seed catalogs and she went to town," Celeste replied. "I don't know how she thinks she's going to grow all these plants in this climate. I told them you're a gardener," she added. "They're excited about growing their own flowers. Flora, tell them this is the man."

Flora obliged, and the girls looked at Keene with astonishment. Najima let go of the knife in her pocket. When Mrs. Celeste had told her that a man would help them plant a garden, she'd expected him to be shrunken, old, unfit for heavier toil. But this man, despite his silver hair, looked vigorous and strong. And he was police. She could not fathom it. Why would he help?

Fadeelah was chattering on about the different kinds of flowers she wanted to grow, with Flora translating and the man talking about his own garden. Flowers as big as your face! Could such a thing be true in this land of cold gray skies? Did the sun ever shine in England? If Fin-sen lived here, would he even be able to see the stars?

But the man was talking to her, asking a question. Najima looked at Flora.

"He wants to know if you've ever used a computer," said Flora.

The Answer Box, with its lines of tiny letters and strange symbols? Najima shook her head, suddenly shy. She could identify a few of the shapes, but it would take a very long time before she would be able to ask a question and read the answer. She hoped in time the Answer Box could tell her how Zainab was faring.

But the man was waiting for her reply. "I must learn to speak and read English first," she told Flora. "Tell him Mrs. Celeste says I will go to school, and I will learn."

His expression softened as he listened to Flora. It was not an expression Najima was used to seeing on a man's face. Zainab used to look that way when Najima did something kind or clever. What did it mean now?

"He says you will be an excellent student because you are smart and brave," Flora told her.

Najima could count on one hand the times a man had praised her. Inside, the baby turned, making her stomach ripple. She groped for the armchair and let herself sink down.

Flora wheeled Fadeelah into the kitchen to help make tea. Fadeelah was a little nervous and a little excited: they were going to serve the first batch of gingersnaps she had made herself (though Mrs. Flora had supervised), and now they would be tasted by the important policeman that Mrs. Celeste seemed to like. This was a crucial test: everyone in the family would tell her the gingersnaps were good because they cared about her feelings (which itself was a thing to wonder at). But would a policeman bother to lie?

Benny brought in extra chairs, and they all squeezed around the kitchen table. The dining room table was bigger, but the kitchen felt cozier. In fact, it reminded Celeste of long-ago Thanksgivings back home. Looking around, she marveled at all the faces. Usually she sat here alone, eating the dinner Flora had left her.

In addition to gingersnaps, Flora served fish-paste sandwiches and scones. When everyone had food on their plate and tea in their cup, an awkward silence settled over the group. Celeste eyed Keene with sympathy. Brits excelled at small talk, but she felt sorry for the poor man. He couldn't ask the girls about their families, or what films they liked, or what profession they planned to pursue. How did you talk to someone who has just been freed from slavery?

But Keene surprised her. Going through Flora, he asked the girls what they liked about ER, which Celeste had mentioned during their verbal game of catch. The answer was immediate.

"Shorsh Ka-loon-ee," the girls said in unison.

And then, just like normal teenagers, they giggled. Celeste's heart expanded—she could actually feel it grow bigger inside her chest.

"George Clooney, one of the stars," she explained to Keene, who followed with other questions until the girls were chattering so fast Flora could hardly keep up: the kind doctors, the children, the terrifying injuries and illnesses, the heroism, and the glimpses they saw of wild exotic America.

When Keene praised the gingersnaps, Fadeelah—at least the half of her that wasn't trapped by a sling or encased in plaster —squirmed with pleasure. Keene asked Benny and Flora about their backgrounds, not as a policeman—though it must have been hard not to revert to interrogation mode—but as an interested guest, a friend of the family. Celeste was absurdly pleased that he showed no sign of class consciousness: it was one of the things she disliked about British society. About any society.

From time to time, Keene's phone rang as his men checked in with progress reports on a handful of cases.

"This reminds me," he said after one of these calls. "Why is it Americans can never just say 'Goodbye'?" The glint in his eyes let Celeste know that he was teasing again. "They say 'Well, good luck with all that, nice talking to you, have a great day, see you soon, take care' and on and on. We British simply say 'Goodbye,' and that's that. But Americans seem oddly reluctant to let one go."

"Well, just 'goodbye' sounds kind of curt," Celeste said. "Kind of cold."

"Ah, there is a difference between 'cold' and 'reserved,'" he replied, and they were off again. The conversation flew back and forth, with the spectators turning their heads as if watching tennis. Fadeelah and Najima laughed when the others did, even if they didn't understand: the merriment was contagious. And welcome.

When the last drop and crumb had disappeared, Keene rose to his feet, thanking Flora and Fadeelah warmly for the feast. Celeste fetched his coat. The event he'd been waiting for had apparently not yet occurred, but she could not manage to feel disappointed.

And at any rate, he came back the very next day. Everyone except Flora seemed surprised. Celeste was so surprised as she opened the door that she forgot what she'd been about to say and instead blurted: "What happened to your mustache?"

Then she flinched. What a rude American! Such a personal remark!

But Keene only grinned and touched the bare skin above his lip. "I remembered what you said about young men growing them to look older, and I wondered if the reverse were true."

He seemed to be waiting for a response, but Celeste could think of nothing more sophisticated to say than: "You do! It is!" He looked brighter, newer, scrubbed. And for some reason, the absence of the mustache made his eyes bluer, though she could hardly tell him that.

Meanwhile, Keene made himself at home in the living room, where Najima was carefully painting henna designs on Fadeelah's uninjured hand. Flora helped Fadeelah explain that traditional Jadali brides all had intricate designs painted on their hands and feet for the wedding, but she thought the swirling patterns might make a pretty cake-top, so she and Najima were practicing. Keene bent down to admire their work. Daringly, Najima offered to decorate one of his own hands, a suggestion which mortified Fadeelah: no man wore henna! But Keene just smiled and said perhaps next time when he wasn't on duty.

Flora made a curry for lunch, and they'd just sat down to eat, crowded around the kitchen table again, when Keene's mobile rang, and he popped back up. He had a low terse exchange with the caller—all Celeste managed to hear was "He landed? He's through?"—then swiveled to face the family again.

"I do apologize, but I'm afraid I must go. An important meeting. We've been waiting for one last person to show up. Well, two people. Well, three."

"They all came at once?" Celeste asked.

"You'll understand after the meeting."

"I'm coming with you?"

"We're Two and Three."

Celeste gawped at him in what she feared was a most unattractive way. Meanwhile, Benny tugged his napkin out of his collar and lumbered to his feet. "I'll get the car, Missus," he said.

Keene stopped him. "That won't be necessary, Mr. Butters," he said gently. "I'll see her safely home when we're through."

Everyone seemed to look at everyone else for an explanation. But Keene was already heading for the door, and Celeste followed, yanking their coats from the closet on the way.

Keene's car, like the man himself, was neat and respectable. Celeste looked for hidden police insignia but saw none. Nor did she see any crushed paper cups, take-away wrappers, scraps of paper, or any other kind of trash. She wondered what the inside of his house looked like. Or his garden. No doubt he was an assiduous weeder. Somehow the notion struck her as endearing.

"You may have noticed," Keene began—she hadn't: she'd been

too busy imagining his house—"that we are not heading to the station. The meeting is being held elsewhere."

"Because of the mole?"

"Indeed. And if they mention him, please remember to be surprised."

"Who is 'they'?"

"My superiors. Their superiors. And other...colleagues."

She started to ask the next question, but he held up one hand. "No more about the case now, all right? Let's wait for the meeting."

"I'm not good at waiting."

"So I gather."

She sighed. "All right, then let me ask you this. Why are the British so abrupt when they say goodbye?"

He cut her a sharp glance. "Very funny."

"Maybe it's because Brits have never learned to appreciate peanut butter and jelly."

She was resuming the game they'd begun in the park. He tried not to grin. "Yes, but we do appreciate Vegemite."

Celeste made a face. "Salty yeast on toast. How about chili dogs?"

"How about bubble-and-squeak?"

"Pecan pie."

"Treacle tart. Are we only going to talk about food?"

"Let's talk about which side of the road it makes more sense to drive on."

The meeting, it turned out, was being held in a tall glass-and-steel office building in a block of tall glass-and-steel office buildings. Celeste kept stepping backward, trying to see the top.

"What is this place?" she asked. "I don't think I've been here before."

Keene caught her elbow before she stepped into the street. "No, you wouldn't have done. The government keeps anonymous offices here for use in sensitive matters."

"You don't want the mole to hear about the meeting."

"You are quick," he said, holding the door open.

Again, Celeste felt absurdly pleased by this observation.

The elevator arrived. She sneaked a sideways glance as the doors opened. He really did look younger without the mustache.

The conference room consisted of a long tableful of men sitting in mustard-yellow vinyl chairs. Celeste thought she recognized one or two faces from the last meeting. She was the only woman.

Keene made a quick round of introductions: there was a Commissioner, a Deputy Commissioner or perhaps an Assistant Deputy Commissioner—it was hard to keep track—a Detective Chief Superintendent, and a Special Branch officer. Celeste wasn't sure what Special Branch did, but, given the British penchant for euphemism, "special" could mean something ominous indeed. One of the dignitaries was so jowly he looked like he had mumps. One had a sad baby-face. Another bore an uncanny resemblance to her high school chemistry teacher. There were also two civilians, men from the Home Office whose matching bald domes, spectacles, and gray suits seemed to echo the glass-and-steel buildings outside. But one other was not introduced. Slight, with round rimless glasses and a beaky little nose, he reminded her of T.S. Eliot. Keene murmured that this was the man they'd been waiting for: he'd flown in overnight from Cyprus.

The jowly man—Mumps—thanked Celeste for coming and for assisting with the case. Then, to her surprise, he turned the meeting over to the unnamed man, who spoke fluent English with a French accent. He was the sort of man whose face you'd forget as soon as you looked away. Was he police? Government? Secret Service?

"We have been following the activities of Tariq Farouqi for the past three years," the small man began. "With assistance, of course, from British, American, and European authorities."

Celeste interrupted: "Who is *we*?" There was no point being considered a rude American if you couldn't act like one.

"Forgive me," said the Frenchman. "I have misplaced the habit of introducing myself. I am Gaspard Gigot, and I work for Interpol."

Celeste tried not to goggle. She had never—as far as she knew—seen an agent of the fabled Internatonal Police.

He leaned across the table as if speaking only to her. "As I was saying, we've had Tariq Farouqi on our radar for quite a while now. Your young friend has been most industrious."

"He's not *my* young friend," Celeste retorted. "I don't think he's *anyone's* young friend."

Then she glared around the table of well-dressed men. What were they implying?

Sad Baby dropped his eyes. Mumps busied himself polishing his glasses. Steel and Glass simply gazed, impassive. Next to her, Keene stirred as if about to reach out a hand.

Celeste turned to him. "Is this a set-up?"

But Inspector Gigot answered with a chuckle. "Not at all, Madame. I expressed myself without elegance. I only meant to say that we have been waiting for an opportunity, a way in."

"And that's me?" Her voice came out squeakier than she liked.

Gigot leaned forward. "Indeed, Madame. This time we think *la souris* will catch *le chat*."

She didn't need to speak French to understand *that.* The mouse will catch the cat. She leaned back with a smile, relaxing. "Well then, boys," she drawled, letting the Texas out. "What can I do to help?"

CHAPTER ELEVEN

"First, tell us everything," said Gigot.

Celeste, trying not to sigh, again recited the details of Najima's story. The men sat as still as if they were hearing it for the first time. "But you know all this," she finished. Again, she looked at Keene. "Why am I here?"

Gigot answered. "Forgive me, Madam. It was I who requested your presence. I needed what you Americans call a gut feel. To make sure you could be trusted."

"Trusted? I'm the one who brought this case to the police!"

"Indeed, but it is a much more complicated case than you know. And we needed to make sure young Monsieur Farouqi had not found a way to…" He swirled his fingers in an elegant Gallic gesture. "Contaminate your testimony."

"Contaminate?" Then she got it. "You mean bribe me?"

Gigot gave her a patient smile. "Or blackmail. He is ambitious, this young man. As you Americans say, he dips the fingers in many pies."

"So why hasn't Interpol arrested him?"

He shrugged. "Interpol itself has no police powers. We collaborate with local authorities, we share information. Until now, we have not been able to pin Monsieur Farouqi down. We have gained access to some of his bank records. We have followed him, monitored his contacts, tapped his phone lines, but what we know is still either speculation or evidence that would not stand up in court." His smile became rueful. "We have not always acquired information by the most…legitimate means. We have had to judge by the effects his activities seem to produce in the criminal world—do you follow?"

"Sure," said Celeste. "Like astronomers inferring the existence of a black hole by its effect on other stars."

Gigot seemed amused. "Yes, just like that, Madame."

Then one of the superiors—Sad Baby—spoke up. "Theory is one thing. Probable cause is another."

"*Exactement*," Gigot replied. "But now, thanks to you, Madame Stoneman, we have a way in. Another avenue of investigation."

"The girls?"

"The girls get us into the house. The house gives us the umbrella. The umbrella leads us to the Sarin, which leads to everything else."

"There's more?"

Gigot glanced at the others as if offering them the chance to speak. Keene, Mumps, Sad Baby, Chemistry Teacher, Glass, and Steel all gazed soberly back. No one wanted the ball.

"Monsieur Farouqi must know we are watching—he is too clever not to suspect—but he seems to take special delight in covering his tracks, disguising his activities with layers of shell companies. They are the gloves that keep his hands clean. It is one of these dummy corporations that outbid the pipe contract your ex-husband organized. That may not have been illegal, but it was—" He paused.

"Unethical," Mumps supplied.

"Malicious," added Glass, while Steel nodded just once.

"*Exactement*. It reveals his true nature. For the last five years, we believe, he has been building a criminal network. Mostly guns and drugs. And money-laundering, of course."

"Is he a terrorist?"

"Not per se—one would need an ideology for that. We think power and wealth are his only ideals. But that doesn't mean he has nothing to do with terrorists. He's made a fortune buying opium from Afghanistani *mujahideen* and selling it to wholesale dealers. He buys Kalashnikovs from the Russians, thus helping to finance their war with Chechnya, then turns around and sells those very weapons to the Chechens. What is the expression? Playing both sides against the middle? We think Russian mafia may be involved as well."

"Oh!" Celeste couldn't help glancing at Keene. "My ex-husband mentioned mysterious streams of Russian money flooding the market."

"The Russians," Sad Baby said morosely, "will be the new Jadalis."

Gigot resumed: "But this Sarin business is an even bigger problem. We assume the subway Tokyo attacks gave Monsieur Farouqi a storm in the head."

"Brainstorm," Mumps corrected.

"Yes, a brainstorm—a unique business opportunity. Sarin is efficient and economical, easier to acquire than guns or opium, easily transported, easily activated. And the profit margin is higher." Gigot shrugged again. "A cost-effective terror weapon. It makes sense. Perhaps he plans to sell it to the clients he already has: the *mujahideen*, the Chechens—who knows?" Gigot glanced pointedly around the table. "Perhaps to the I.R.A."

Sad Baby sighed. Glass and Steel looked grim.

"But even with all this surveillance," Celeste persisted, "you still don't have enough to arrest him?"

Mumps spoke up: "It's absurdly easy to hide large amounts of cash: all you need is a post office box and an email address. You buy high-end goods and services, paying thirty times what they're worth, and you invest in small businesses that exist only to provide a facade: launderettes, pawn shops, nail salons, nightclubs."

Celeste remembered Tariq's invitation to the VIP room at his nightclub, how uncomfortable it made her feel. He'd been mocking her. Secretly laughing up his well-tailored sleeve. A lot of women might fall for that.

"You transfer funds from one dummy corporation to another," Mumps continued, "establishing anonymous accounts in places like the Seychelles, Hong Kong, Cyprus, Belize, easing the way with bribes and low-interest 'loans' which are promptly forgiven."

"We think he uses a network of cash mules," said Gigot. "Specializing in flight attendants." He leaned forward: "We have been watching for a long time. He is very careful, but we think he must suspect: some of his activities seem like taunts. The pipe contract, for instance."

"I don't really understand that," said Celeste.

Gigot spread his hands wide. "He wishes, as you say, to stick it to his father. The father will unknowingly pay the son for the contract. It is a feather in the cap. He has a history of such private swindles."

"His case file's as thick as the Bible," Sad Baby muttered.

"Thus far we have been calling this operation Traffik Games," Gigot continued. "Young Monsieur Farouqi evidently considers himself a master player. We wish," he added pleasantly, "to demonstrate that he is mistaken."

"Is his father involved?"

"We think not. Muhktar Farouqi may be sunk in corruption up to his neck in Jadal—in bed, as you say, with the royal family—but that is a Jadali matter and does not concern us. And whatever else one might say about him, Muhktar seems genuinely devout. He would find many of Tariq's activities repellent—investing in insurance companies, for example. The insurance business does not exist in Jadal: it is considered sacrilegious since everything is willed by God."

Celeste's eyes narrowed. A God who wills human slavery? Rape? Female mutilation? But she only repeated her earlier question: "What can I do to help?"

She was a civilian, after all, and had already told them, multiple times, everything she knew. Did they want to stage a sting, perhaps? They could use her as bait, but she wouldn't risk the girls.

"I am glad that you ask, Madame," Gigot answered. "You must do nothing, please."

"Pardon?"

"Madame, I am *désolé*—" He laid a hand briefly over his heart. "I know it is a most difficult, most inconvenient, thing to ask, but we wish for you, the girls, and your staff to remain inside the home. Not to venture out. Not to communicate in any way with the Farouqis. Not to expose yourself to public view. Not to make yourselves vulnerable."

"But we are vulnerable. We're sitting ducks."

Now it was Gigot's turn to ask: "Pardon? Ducks who sit?"

"*Cibles faciles*," Keene said. Celeste turned to look because it was the first time he'd spoken, and she was impressed that he knew the French. "Easy targets."

"Ah yes, of course. Not to worry, Madame. We will maintain the surveillance of your house."

"We've had men watching around the clock," Mumps added.

"Really?" said Celeste. "Men, plural?" She could see Keene's ears turn pink. "Your men are really good. I don't think I've noticed more than, say, one."

"They are well-trained and disciplined," Mumps replied. "We will not lift the surveillance until Tariq Farouqi has been apprehended."

"So, you want us all quarantined in the meantime."

"*Exactement*," said Gigot. "Quarantined, yes."

"For how long? Are we talking hours? Days? Weeks?"

"Not long. We are conducting an…operation which should be resolved within a short time. That is why we seek your full cooperation."

"Another operation?" Celeste was confused. Weren't they already conducting an operation called Traffik Games?

Keene spoke again. "She knows about the mole," he said flatly, and Celeste couldn't help gasping. She would have taken that secret to the grave.

All the men stared at Keene, whose face showed no expression though his ears grew pinker.

"Actually, I figured it out myself," Celeste hastened to add. "I guessed and saw by his face I was right."

Gigot's eyes were half-shut as he pressed the tips of his fingers together. "And just what do you know, Madame?"

"She knows we're going to contrive—"

"Detective Chief Inspector," Gigot interrupted. "I would like to hear from the lady herself."

Contrive. What would they contrive? A test of some sort.

"A test," she said. "You're going to dangle some bait and see who grabs it."

Gigot seemed pleased. "Indeed, Madame. Are you certain you have no police experience yourself?"

"No, I'm just naturally sneaky."

"So we have heard," Sad Baby said dryly. "You have a penchant for masquerade, apparently."

Celeste felt her own cheeks heat. "Well, Halloween is my favorite holiday," she said, even though it wasn't: her favorite was Thanksgiving.

"So yes," Gigot continued. "We will feed false information to the men we suspect and see who acts upon it. This is a very sensitive operation in many ways, Madame. Quite frankly, we hope to avoid a political and media *merdier.*"

Though Celeste didn't speak French, she didn't need to ask for a translation: everyone knew what *merde* meant. Gigot was talking about a shitstorm, a term not unfamiliar to Texans.

"Only the officers at this table know about it. And now you," he added.

Did he sound a bit dubious? She quickly reassured him. "I understand. That's why you want us quarantined. So no word can possibly get out."

"And for your own protection. That is why you are here—so you can fully appreciate what is at stake."

"I thought it was because you had to see if you could trust me."

"That as well. We must have your complete cooperation, Madame. Your people's safety depends upon it."

"Got it. We all have measles and nobody's going anywhere."

"Pardon? Meez-alls?"

"*Rougeole,*" Keene put in, impressing Celeste again.

"Ah," said Gigot, leaning back in satisfaction. Apparently, she amused the forgettable little man.

"DCI Keene will keep you informed," Mumps went on. "But the quarantine must remain in place until you get the all-clear."

"I understand," said Celeste as the men stood up.

"Be vigilant, Madame," Gigot said. "Take no risks."

"Right." She restrained the urge to salute. "Good luck, guys."

They stared blankly back. Maybe you weren't supposed to wish the police luck—maybe, like theater people, they said Break a Leg? An image of Tariq hurling Fadeelah from the balcony flashed through her mind, followed by the memory of Begum beating a starved pregnant teenager. Fadeelah's and Najima's bruises were starting to fade, but the two girls still enslaved would have fresh ones. She studied the roomful of men waiting for her to leave and let her eyes harden.

"Shut him down, gentlemen," she said. "Shut him down."

Then Keene was cupping her elbow, guiding her from the room as the men sat back down, ready to continue their briefing.

"Well done," he murmured. Apparently, she'd been the pre-game show, and now it was halftime.

"Are there really more constables watching my house?" Celeste asked on the way home.

"Uh...yes." Keene frowned at a BMW trying to wedge itself into a tiny parking spot.

"And they've been there all along?"

He sighed, resigning himself to the truth. "Since the night of the attack."

"So, you really didn't need to be there personally." It wasn't a question. "Why were you?"

"I have taken a personal interest," he said with precise dignity, "in the plight of these young women. Drugs and guns are one thing. Human bondage is another."

Celeste hid a smile so he wouldn't see how much she

enjoyed discomfiting him. "So, will you continue monitoring us? Personally?"

Keene rubbed his lip where the mustache used to be. Other than the ears, it was his only tell. "Najima and Fadeelah are important witnesses, and they are extremely vulnerable."

"I guess that means yes," she said and decided to take pity on him. "So, who do your bosses like for the mole?"

He seized the change of subject as if it were a lifebuoy. "Three men have unexpectedly come into money. One just returned from a trip to Bali. Another bought a lovely holiday home in the Cotswolds. And the third is driving a jaunty little Jaguar, brand new." He shook his head. "Not likely on a policeman's salary, I can tell you that."

"What's the trap?"

"That I can't tell you."

"Who are the suspects?"

"Can't give you any names. It's a precarious situation."

"Who am I going to tell? My fellow prisoners? We're all under house arrest, remember?" She turned in her seat to face him. "Did Gigot really want me there so he could size me up?"

They stopped at a traffic light, so he faced her. "Gigot is an old spy. They are like dogs who can sense when a human has cancer or diabetes long before the human is aware. When Gigot leans toward you, it's not to make a point—it's to observe your body language, to see whether your pupils enlarge, whether you glance to your left."

"Whether I'm lying."

"Precisely."

"So, I passed the test?"

"Of course. As I said, the situation is fragile. The slightest lapse could make it fall apart. We wanted to be sure you understood that we are moving on the Farouqis even if it doesn't look that way. We wanted you to take precautions, stay put, keep safe where we can watch." He glanced at her. "It was actually I who suggested you attend, and Gigot agreed. We had to make sure you would trust us to protect you and the girls."

"You didn't trust me to trust you?" Hearing the sulkiness in her voice, she winced. Goodness, she was reverting to her teenage self. Was that the effect Keene had on her? "Sorry," she muttered. "I do appreciate your efforts. We all do."

At this, Keene relaxed his grip on the steering wheel. "My turn to change the subject. Fancy a picnic?"

"Picnic?" Celeste glanced out at the freezing rain. "I'm not supposed to leave the house, remember?"

"That's where the picnic will be," he replied. "After one quick stop."

"What's this? Father Christmas?" Benny cried as they struggled through the door with their stout shopping bags.

"Just as well might be," said Flora, coming to help. "You went to Harrods?"

"Ask the lunatic," said Celeste. "All his idea."

"We need a blanket," Keene added. "For the picnic."

Celeste and Flora exchanged looks which meant something like: *Can you believe this*? And: *You bet I can*!

Soon the blanket was spread on the living room floor. Najima wheeled Fadeelah's chair right up to the edge, then dragged a kitchen chair over for herself—even if she made it all the way down, she would never be able to haul herself back up. Flora brought in plates and cutlery as Benny pulled things out of the shopping bags, announcing them in a tone of steadily increasing astonishment: three kinds of cheese, including his favorite, Welsh Y Fenni, made with mustard seed and ale; plus cured duck confit, lamb terrine, quail eggs, white asparagus, three kinds of olives, loaves of focaccia and sourdough, onion marmalade, pickled mushrooms, small sweet strawberries—strawberry was still Najima's favorite flavor—tiny champagne grapes, a jug of Suffolk cider, and a splendid crème cake, decorated with spun-sugar flowers and presented directly to Fadeelah, who gasped.

"He insisted," Celeste told them, dishing out the goods. "I told him there's no need—"

"But there is," Keene interrupted. "You've been feeding me like a prince. It was time to return the favor."

Benny tucked in without hesitation, and Celeste was pleased to see that both girls took a nibble of everything, not that any of it stood a chance against ice cream.

While they ate, Celeste described the meeting, amusing Keene with her impressions of Sad Baby, Mumps, Chemistry Teacher, Steel, and Glass. He conceded it was easier than remembering actual names or rank. Celeste had never seen him smile so much. How could she have ever thought him impassive? Suit coat off, tie rolled up and stored in the pocket, he reclined at ease on the blanket, laughing and chatting, sharing bits of things with the girls and accepting bits from them. Celeste had never actually celebrated Christmas—it wasn't her holiday—but if this was what it was like, she might have to start. All they needed was a Tiny Tim to declare: "God bless us, every one!" Fadeelah already had the crutch!

And they were blessed, weren't they?

But then she remembered the other two girls still enslaved, with no idea rescue was coming, and suddenly the strawberries didn't taste so sweet.

Just as they were finishing, Keene received a brief call. He said very little but nodded at Celeste when he rang off.

"It's on," he said. The trap was set.

Celeste had told the others about the quarantine but she hadn't mentioned the mole. No point in giving them more to worry about. But she thought it was going to be a very long night. And a very long day tomorrow, if something didn't happen soon. She wondered how long Keene would stay. Might he be planning to spend the night? They were safe enough—if Mumps was right, police were guarding the house at this very moment. Then again, the second guest room was already made up. Did Keene prefer coffee or tea for breakfast? Of course, they could always make both.

After the feast, Flora and Celeste cleaned up while Benny and

Keene showed the girls how to build a house from a deck of cards. The frequent bursts of laughter told Celeste they were not having as much success as one might hope. Yet the language barrier seemed to present no problem.

She called Elaine and Abby to bring them up to date. Both wanted to come over immediately and pelt Keene with questions, but she told them no one but Keene could come and go. She did not mention the mole. They both made her promise to call them the minute something happened. Willow said the same when Celeste finally reached her in Milan. They had all played important roles in this bizarre operation, and they wanted to be there for the finish. They wanted to see the cops take Tariq down.

When the girls started yawning, Celeste, awkward as a teenager, asked Keene if he'd like to stay over in the guest room.

"Thank you, but that won't be necessary. Besides," he added, not quite smiling, "I haven't got my toothbrush."

"I have an extra," Celeste said quickly, then flinched. She hadn't meant to sound eager.

His gaze was warm as it rested on her. "No need. I'll just have a word with the surveillance team before I go."

Did the man ever sleep? "Then you'll go straight home? Get some rest?"

"Yes, but I'll be on call for the rest of the night, so if you need anything…"

"We need you to get some sleep, Charles!"

Grinning now, he wished everyone good night and accepted his coat from Celeste. He had just put his hand on the doorknob when his mobile rang. Celeste held her breath, hoping he wouldn't take the call outside. This conversation was also very brief.

He listened a moment, then barked: "On my way."

Still holding the phone to his ear, he faced the others. "Surveillance says the Farouqis are on the move. Heading for the airfield and their private jet. We've got to catch them before they get on that plane." His voice became very firm. "I want you all to stay put, stay inside. Now is no time to—" He broke off. Celeste was pulling her coat from the closet. "What are you doing?"

"Coming with you."

"No, you can't—"

"We'll be right behind you, Missus!" Benny cried, jingling his keys.

"No civilians! You must all stay put," Keene told Celeste.

She took a step closer. "Listen to me, Detective Chief Inspector Keene," she said, uncorking the Texas. "I would rather eat a bowlful of bees."

"This could cost me my job," he muttered.

"Surely not! Not after we catch him!"

He snorted at the we, then shrugged, resigned. "I suppose you'd just follow me anyway."

Celeste wasted no time. "Call Abby and Elaine!" she told Flora, throwing on her coat. "Let them know what's going on!"

"Tell them to stay home!" Keene added.

"Shortest quarantine ever!" Benny crowed, as Celeste yanked the door shut and they hurried to Keene's car.

From nowhere—under the seat? in the glove box?—he pulled out a blue light dome, fixed it to the dashboard, set it flashing, then clipped on the police radio. Celeste tightened her seatbelt. Keene took off, driving like a highly skilled maniac, hands clenched on the wheel. Now it was a race.

"Do you know who the mole is?" Celeste asked when she caught her breath.

"We do," he said grimly. "One of them was just placed under arrest."

"One of them?"

He shot her a glance. "The holiday home in the Cotswolds was bought by a gambler who had a bit of luck at the tables. The second man, the one who went to Bali, has apparently acquired wealthy in-laws who covered all expenses. That leaves the third

—"

He broke off to listen to the radio and mutter a quick response.

"The third?" Celeste pressed.

"Your friend the sergeant."

"Barnett." The red-headed bully who scoffed at her claims. Now it made sense: he worked for Tariq. She didn't know why she felt shocked—perhaps because she had not often experienced betrayal.

"We've been following him for a while. Today we released some crucial disinformation: we told the gambler and the son-in-law that this operation was being suspended due to lack of evidence, but we let Barnett 'overhear' the Deputy Commissioner—Mumps—" he suppressed a grin—"confirm that we planned to move on the Farouqis at dawn. Shortly thereafter, Barnett developed a toothache and asked leave to visit the dentist. We followed him, of course. Instead of the dentist, he went to a callbox and conducted a brief but agitated conversation."

"Tariq."

"We assume. We'll know for certain after we check the call records."

"He was warning Tariq about the dawn raid?"

He gave her a single nod. "Which is why the family is scrambling to get out now. The surveillance team reports some kind of disturbance in the house—lots of movement, raised voices, all the cars brought round front." He paused to listen to his radio, said "Right," then told Celeste: "Apparently Tariq just came screeching up the drive and ran into the house."

"He's very careless with that Lamborghini," Celeste murmured, remembering the night of the gala. "But even if we get there on time, how will you stop them?"

"SO19 are on the scene. Tactical Forces." He glanced at her. "They have guns."

"Oh!" This also shocked her. She hadn't imagined gunfire and blood.

"Special Branch are there as well," Keene continued.

"What, the Beefeaters couldn't make it?"

He smiled as if he knew that Celeste made wisecracks when she was nervous. Of course, she made wisecracks when she wasn't nervous as well. Perhaps he knew that too.

Then she remembered. "You said one of them."

"We detained someone else en route to Heathrow." He glanced at her, taking his time. Was he actually enjoying himself? "Someone who had no idea we were watching him. Someone who used Barnett as his henchman while he directed things from the top. Someone who did not want to lose his lucrative side gig."

"Someone?"

"Deputy Assistant Commissioner of Metropolitan Police." He raised his eyebrows. "I believe you know him as Sad Baby?"

"Sad Baby!" Celeste gasped, remembering the doleful face and chubby cheeks. Somehow, they made the news even more disturbing.

"Yes, Tariq Farouqi's silent partner, as it were. That's how Tariq was able to stay one step ahead of the law for so long. But we've got him now," he added cheerfully.

Keene's radio crackled again. He responded briefly, then stopped talking to concentrate on rocketing down the motorway. Celeste pictured Benny and Flora and the girls riding his tailwind as he veered onto the shoulder, cut corners, ran lights. She shut her eyes so she wouldn't see the near-misses—she had never been in a car traveling this fast—and hoped that if the others were indeed following, they would arrive after Tariq was in custody. She hadn't rescued those girls only to see them get shot. Then she heard sirens up ahead and stopped thinking altogether.

CHAPTER TWELVE

The first thing Muhktar did after Tariq's call was to telephone his platoon of lawyers. Next, he told his wives.

"Pack a few essential things," he said. "We leave within the hour."

Begum panicked. "Tariq?"

"He's on his way. Now go. Hurry."

Mehraj turned obediently, but Begum, who was first wife and older, paused to pluck at her husband's sleeve. "But why?" she asked. "Why must we rush?"

Muhktar would have liked an answer to that question as well, but it would have to wait. "We have enemies," he said darkly, removing her hand. She bowed her head and followed Mehraj up the stairs.

Muhktar had also panicked when Tariq told him they had to flee, though it didn't manifest in his face or voice—only his fingers gave him away: he couldn't stop tugging his beard, like a young man trying to make it grow faster. He didn't want to leave London, at least not until his people figured out what was holding up the pipe contract, but he trusted his son. The important thing right now was to get his family out of Britain, go home, beyond the reach of Western law. The Tribe. You always returned to the Tribe because the Tribe would always protect you. There would be time enough to talk in Jadal.

◆ ◆ ◆

Begum and Mehraj were profoundly annoyed. Jameela and Dafiyah would pack for the children, but the wives had to pack their own belongings. They were short-staffed because of that interfering *Amreekiyah*, who they should never have invited over for coffee. Talk about letting the camel poke his nose in your tent!

And they were cross with their husband as well. Muhktar had followed them up the stairs to propose leaving the two maids with the skeleton staff staying behind to protect *Hadiqa House*: he called them extra baggage! This time both Mehraj and Begum whirled around indignantly. Mehraj was especially horrified: imagine having to care for three children all by herself! And Begum actually lectured her husband: the maids were their property; the Farouqis had paid for them; they needed them.

Muhktar rapidly reconsidered: after all, he didn't want the girls talking to the police. But mainly, Begum was right: Farouqis kept what belonged to them. He left his wives and hurried downstairs to the vault. There wasn't time to wrap up his most valuable antiquities: he would have to choose a precious few to carry with him on the plane. Now that would be a hard decision.

Mehraj and Begum did not need to discuss priorities. They rushed to their dressing rooms to pack up their cherished Western cosmetics—the new brand they'd discovered, Willow, worked miracles with tiny lines. But Mehraj's hands were shaking; she dropped the nearly full bottle of Strategy. A cloud of expensive stink soaked the thick carpet and seemed to intensify with their grumbling.

Muhktar struggled to open the vault. He'd punched in the right code, but his physical strength had deserted him. The lifelike cobra guarding the massive door seemed to sneer. Could snakes sneer? He shook his head, blotted his face with his sleeve, and stepped inside, where he lost precious minutes hesitating over what to choose. So much was irreplaceable! The black obsidian bowl, rumored to be 5000 years old—he remembered how difficult it was to acquire, how many go-betweens and bribes it took. But was it more valuable—personally, to him—than the cuneiform tablets? The lapis lazuli baby rattle, which had belonged to an ancient king's son? The daggers in their jeweled sheaths? The star maps?

Ordinarily, Muhktar never dithered, but he hovered over one artifact after another, opening cases and drawers, trying to hear what spoke loudest. But when he opened the drawer with the astrolabe, everything went still. He remembered that the word meant "the one who catches the heavenly bodies." A star-tracker, the navigation instrument his ancestors had used to find their way home. Reverently, he wrapped the ancient bronze disk in layers of padding and stowed it in his briefcase. He was so engrossed that he actually jumped when his son spoke behind him.

"What are you doing, *Abi?* We need to go," said Tariq.

"I wanted to—I thought—" Muhktar gave his head a hard shake, trying to focus. What was the matter with him? He was doddering like an old man. "Just a little something in case..."

Tariq smiled. He didn't seem rattled a bit.

"Go on, *Abi*," he said, clapping his father's shoulder. "Get those women moving. Wheels up in thirty minutes."

Muhktar nodded rapidly, took one last blind look, and hurried out, leaving his treasures behind.

Alone in the vault, Tariq gave the treasures no more than a glance. For an instant he pictured his ancestors, the *Bedu* warriors who galloped the desert, rifles slung over their backs. They would recognize him, those warriors. They would acknowledge his kinship, salute him as a sheik. Then he had to indulge himself in a brief chuckle. How far would you get in the

West with a rifle on your back? He considered bringing a dagger, but there was already something in his pocket that would, if necessary, prove far more useful. So, he grabbed the one object that really mattered to him and raced after his father, overtaking him on the stairs.

The women, children, and staff had clustered in the front hall, spilling outside to the drive where the SUVs and limo waited. Tariq glanced at them with distaste. He'd considered commandeering the family jet, leaving everyone behind, but decided against it: partly because of his tribal instincts but mostly because he suspected the crew would only take orders from his father. That was something he would rectify when they got back to Jadal.

Muhktar staggered to the top of the stairs, uncharacteristically embarrassed because he could not control his panting. He barely noticed the members of his household. His eyes were fixed on his son. Of all the treasures in the vault, Tariq had chosen the umbrella? Yes, it was raining, but—

"Everyone into the cars!" Tariq ordered, and the crowd surged forward, not even noticing that they jostled the sheik as they passed. And so, the Farouqis abandoned *Bayt Hadiqa*, House of Gardens.

Keene and Celeste were still twenty minutes out from the airfield when the *Nee-Naw, Nee-Naw*—so unlike an American siren's wail—abruptly cut off. Celeste peered through drizzle at blurry flashing lights, blue and red: police cars, two ambulances, a fire truck, and a bulky heap blocking the motorway.

"Dear God," she said. "What happened?"

The bulky heap was actually five or six piled-up automobiles that had skidded in the rain and crashed, one after the other. A chain reaction. And now the mess, along with all the emergency vehicles, was blocking the road. Traffic had stopped. The road had become a four-lane parking lot.

Keene swore softly as he leaped out and approached the officer in charge. He showed his warrant card, exchanged a few hasty words, then waited impatiently as the officer spoke into his radio. The officer nodded, then jumped into the nearest police car.

"Follow me!" he ordered. "Stay close!"

Lights still flashing, he took off. Keene jumped back into his own car and gunned the engine. Celeste hugged her purse—there was nothing else to hold onto. Keene followed the police car as it cut back around the pile-up, then pulled onto the grassy median. It led them past all the mess, bumping hard along the dips and hollows. Keene's face was grim as he peered over the steering wheel, trying to will better visibility. Celeste desperately wanted to crack a dumb joke—*Are we there yet?*—but luckily the car hit a ditch, bouncing so hard her head smacked the roof.

"Are you hurt?" Keene shouted, extending his arm a moment too late.

"I'm fine!" she yelled back, not sure why they were yelling, except that it seemed necessary. "Just drive!"

When they finally cleared the roadblock, their escort gave them a wave and made a U-turn, racing back toward the accident. Keene pulled the car onto the road with a sickening metal crunch, then stepped hard on the gas. They had lost precious minutes. The Farouqis could be boarding their plane at this very moment. So instead of a stupid joke, Celeste settled for just saying something stupid: "Can't you go any faster?"

Najima thought that Mr. Benny drove like a sand devil, one of those sudden storms that rose up and blanked out the rest of the world. She held tight to Fadeelah's good hand as they struggled to keep their balance in the bulleting car. She could tell Fadeelah was in pain, but she'd refused to be left behind, and there was no time to argue. Mr. Benny had basically heaved her into the car along with her crutches and taken off almost before Najima got their door shut. The ride would have been thrilling if they weren't so terrified.

But Najima was not terrified of Mr. Tariq anymore, nor the sheik, nor the wives, nor any other member of that household. She had her knife, and if any of them got close enough—if they tried to hurt Dafiyah or Jameela—that blade would taste Farouqi blood. She hoped the girls would recover from the shock. Rescue had been scary for both Najima and Fadeelah, but it offered new life. And any birth began in pain and violence, did it not?

Fadeelah clenched her teeth against the throbbing in her leg and prayed for Dafiyah and Jameela, for Mrs. Celeste and Mrs. Flora and Mr. Benny, for Najima's baby, the midwife, the kind policeman, and all the others she newly loved. She no longer worried that the Farouqis would attempt to reclaim their property: her new tribe would protect her.

The airport spread out before them like a concrete desert. Celeste spotted her own car slanted near the tall security fence. Benny and Flora were already here? How had they beaten Keene? Probably one of Benny's cabbie friends had warned him about the roadblock—cabbies knew every back road and shortcut, and most of them had police scanners.

Keene pulled right up to the fence, headlamps misting in the darkness. On the other side, police cars clustered in a barricade, green runway lights conferring a festive atmosphere.

Ripping off his seatbelt, Keene barked: "Stay here!"

"Right!" Celeste barked back, then popped out of the car before he did.

Beyond the small terminal, an idling jet waited, along

with the hulks of the Farouqi SUVs, but she couldn't spot their limousine—too many cops in the way. Something was happening out there. You could almost see it: a disturbance in the rain and wind.

They had to go through the small terminal to reach the runway. A skinny young constable, acne still dotting his face, had been left to guard the doors. Keene showed his badge and raced through, but the constable stopped Celeste.

"No more civilians," he said.

"I'm the translator," said Celeste.

He looked confused. "But the other lady just went in."

She didn't hesitate. "I'm the second one. They need us both."

As the young constable frowned, ruminating, she put her Primary Principle into action once more, whisking past out onto the tarmac. Scraping back her hair, she looked for Flora and the girls. Instead, she recognized Abby and Elaine from behind and rushed toward them.

"What are you doing here?" she cried when she spun them around. An idiotic question, but it just popped out.

"Flora called us," Abby said. "And we didn't want to miss a moment."

"It's not entertainment," Elaine muttered in her gravelly voice. "We care, that's all."

No one pointed out that you could care from a safe distance.

"Where are Flora and Benny? And the girls?"

Elaine looked around. "We just saw them a minute ago."

"The press is here too," said Abby, pointing out the news vans, cameras, and microphones crowded against the fence.

So, Willow had kept her promise and made the calls. Celeste tried to take a deep breath. She felt like a shaken bottle of champagne.

"What about Dafiyah and Jameela?" They would be equally terrified of both Farouqis and police.

"Haven't seen them yet," Elaine said, "but the rest of the staff seems to be out of the SUVs."

Police officers crouched behind the barricade of squad cars.

Celeste assumed these were SO19, the SWAT team. They had formed a blockade around two SUV's, which had been left running, doors still open. The jet rumbled. Its stairs had been lowered. Could the Farouqis still escape, make a run for it? Would the plane plow right through the blockade? Would the cops try to shoot it down? Was that even possible?

As the wind dropped, she could hear a cop using a bullhorn to address the clump of servants and security staff. He was ordering them to lay down their weapons, drop to their knees, link their hands behind their heads. "Do it now!" he kept demanding. She was sure there were guns pointed at the Jadalis.

After a good deal of shuffling and exchanging glances, the staff began to comply. As they dropped to their knees one by one, revealing the shiny wet limousine, Celeste spotted Dafiyah and Jameela. She recognized the beefy security guard gripping each of them by the arm—he was the same man who'd escorted her to the bathroom the day she visited *Hadiqa House*. He'd probably been reprimanded for letting her give him the slip. And he was probably gripping the girls harder than he needed to. Their heads hung down. Celeste couldn't see their faces. If she could get close enough, she would commit the unthinkable: rip off her shoes and hurl them at the sheik's face, yank his beard, tear off his *keffiyeh*: contaminate him with female touch. She would tackle Tariq like a linebacker, put her shoulder into it, take him down. He wasn't that big. No matter what, those girls were not getting on that plane.

Najima recognized the big guard: he was one of those who enjoyed handling the girls roughly. While the police were busy corralling and cuffing the other servants, he kept drifting to the back of the group, pulling the two maids along. Najima edged forward. Was he going to make a run for the gate? Maybe use the girls as a shield?

Now and then a cop looked over at the civilians and shouted:

"Get back! Back along the fence!" The civilians took a couple of steps back, then when the cop turned around, edged forward again. Channeling her fourth-grade self, Celeste crouched down and duck-walked through the crowd. If police attention hadn't been focused elsewhere, it wouldn't have been so easy. When she finally risked standing up, she was nearly knocked over by Elaine and Abby, who had glued themselves to her coattails. But at last she spotted Benny supporting Fadeelah, who leaned on one crutch, and Flora clutching an armful of blankets. Najima was with them, but she'd taken a few steps forward. As police cuffed and removed the staff, the silhouettes of Mehraj and the sheik were revealed, one shapely and one stout, wet robes plastered to their bodies. But why were they so still? Why didn't the cops move in? Where were Tariq and Begum?

Bodies shifted, and now Celeste realized what—or rather, who—Najima was inching toward: the guard holding her friends. Was she going to do something reckless? Did she still have that knife? Celeste knew the blade made Najima feel more secure, but would she really use it? She'd used the scissors.

The police were paying no attention to Dafiyah and Jameela. One thing Najima had learned in this cold bleak country was that captives—the powerless—had to rescue themselves. So it was up to her: she would plunge her knife into the guard's back, he would instinctively let go of the girls, and Najima would grab them, pull them to safety. If the police interfered, she would stab them as well. But not the nice policeman who was Mrs. Celeste's friend. It felt as if he were her friend too, even though common sense told her that wasn't possible. Where she came from, police protected the strong, not the weak.

Celeste saw Najima wriggle the knife from the pocket stretched tight over her belly. The delay was just long enough for Celeste to grab her from behind, pinning her arms and squeezing her fingers till they loosened, and the knife dropped to the ground. Celeste kicked it away. It was a good knife, and Flora might kill her for breaking up the set, but she'd have to find a different blade to do it with. That one was staying gone.

She kept holding Najima, who was now crying furious tears and calling her friends' names. Over her head, Celeste spotted Tariq at last, backing away from the limousine, pointing an umbrella like a javelin at the cops. Could that be *the* umbrella? But surely he hadn't had time to arm it. This had to be a trick. Still, police attention was fixed on him.

Now she could see Begum, lumpy in her saturated robes, reaching out a hand to pacify her son. But Tariq, stepping back and cocking his arm, hurled the umbrella at the cops, making them scatter and duck. Instantly he hooked an arm around Begum's throat, yanking her against him.

"Gun!" shouted several cops.

Celeste stared, blinking the rain away. It was true—a pistol had appeared out of nowhere, and he was pressing it to his mother's head.

"Stay back!" he called, voice hoarse.

Was the gun shaking? It was the first time Celeste had ever seen Tariq even slightly unnerved. No doubt that made him more dangerous. He began backing away, dragging his mother with him. Celeste could see Begum paw at Tariq's arm. She seemed to be choking.

Flora's voice broke the spell. "It's a bluff!" she cried. "No Jadali son would ever shoot his mother—it's a bluff!"

Tariq heard her too. "Try me!" he spat.

The police pressed forward. Everyone else fell back, eyes fixed on Tariq. Even his own men stood frozen, staring.

Still in Celeste's arms, Najima lurched forward. Celeste understood immediately and moved with her. They each seized one of the captive girls and yanked their arms free, hauling them backward to safety. The big guard, watching Tariq, scarcely seemed to notice. Nor did the girls resist. Either they'd recognized Najima or decided any fate was better than what the Farouqis had in mind. When they were safe behind the barricade, Najima flung her arms around them and all three burst into tears. Flora popped up beside them, wrapping sodden blankets around their shoulders, murmuring comfort. Benny turned support of Fadeelah over to Abby and Elaine and managed to insert his bulk between the girls and their captors.

Everyone else was still focused on Tariq, who slowly stepped backward, forcing Begum with him as the cops reluctantly made way. Was he going to make a run for the jet stairs? Hold the gun to the pilot's head and say: "Take off now"?

As if reading her mind, Tariq suddenly gave his mother a hard shove. She fell to her hands and knees, gasping. Cops rushed forward to grab her. Tariq, taking advantage of the chaos, turned to run. He didn't see the two cops crouching in the shadow of the plane's wing.

"Drop your weapon!" they yelled. "Hands in the air! Do it now!"

Tariq spun around, snarling. Bedraggled, furious, no longer the well-dressed self-possessed heir to a great fortune, he didn't seem to know where to point his gun.

Muhktar staggered forward. "My son!" he cried just as the crouching cops dove at Tariq's legs. The gun went off. Muhktar fell to the ground, clutching his shoulder. He was instantly surrounded by cops and paramedics.

Begum wailed.

Tariq, immobilized, let out a howl of rage. Then police surrounded him, blocking the view.

Celeste shuddered at the violence. He was down. It was over. A reckless joy swept through her. She wanted to gloat—she wanted to rub it in, to heckle him.

Flora spoke rapidly to all four girls, who stared in astonishment at the sight of Tariq in handcuffs, of Muhktar being loaded into an ambulance. It seemed to knock something loose in them: Najima suddenly threw back her head and began ululating. The other girls instantly followed. The raw trill coming from the backs of their throats—the traditional Arab sound of intense female emotion—gave Celeste chills. Chills on top of chills, since she was freezing. Ignoring the discomfort, she threw back her own head and joined in. So did Flora, then Abby, then Elaine. The women stood in a defiant knot and howled at the sky.

But before Tariq vanished into the squad car, Celeste could not resist giving him the New York equivalent as well: she cupped her hands and yelled: "Game over, asshole!" Let everyone wonder who the obnoxious American was.

Flora translated and the girls laughed out loud. It was a good sound to hear.

As the crime scene tape went up and police cars began clearing out, Celeste spotted Keene. He was talking to Mumps and—was that Monsieur Gigot? He seemed the right size, but even as she watched, he stepped back into shadow. Keene glanced up, catching her eye, and came straight over.

"Everyone all right?" he asked.

"I think so. Will Muhktar recover?"

"From the bullet wound, no doubt. From other wounds, who knows?" He shook hands with everyone and let himself be introduced to Dafiyah and Jameela, who seemed to panic when he extended his hand, refusing to meet his eyes.

"What happens now?" asked Celeste.

"We'll get these girls checked out at A&E," he said, "and then see if we can get them released into your care until their status is sorted."

"I'm coming too," said Flora firmly. "You'll need a translator."

And from the way Najima clung to both girls' hands, it was obvious she was going as well. That was good: the girls could talk through Flora, but they needed a familiar face too. Celeste remembered Fadeelah's terror when the women invaded her hospital room, the time it had taken to gain her trust, something which, in retrospect, made her admire Najima's courage more than ever: she'd trusted Celeste even before Flora, before Fadeelah. She'd taken a blind leap of faith.

"Benny, will you take Fadeelah home? Make sure she puts on dry clothes?" she asked. "I want to ride with Abby and Elaine."

"Right, Missus!" he replied. "Then I'll nip back and fetch the girls, shall I?"

Celeste smiled: Flora was included in that "girls." She was impressed all over again with Benny's sweetness and decency. He and Flora were just as much heroes as the cops who had taken Tariq down.

Keene answered him. "No need. We'll see them home. Mrs. Butters and Najima will keep an eye on them till then. We'll get everyone dry clothes at hospital—if you don't mind scrubs," he added, looking puzzled when the women laughed. Turning to go, he touched Celeste's elbow and said "Cheers."

"Isn't that a toast?"

He smiled, eyes warming. "It also means I'll see you soon."

Celeste wanted to say *I can't thank you enough* but then Keene would reply *Just doing my job, ma'am*. They'd both seen the same movies. But when he held her gaze for a moment before turning away, she saw that the words weren't necessary. She would see him soon.

After the others departed, leaving a handful of officers to preserve the scene, Celeste, Abby, and Elaine sloshed to the gate in their ruined shoes, feet actually squelching. They were really feeling it now—the kind of exhaustion that hits you after a prolonged burst of adrenaline. Everyone would sleep well tonight.

When they reached the parking lot, they heard the roar and whine of another jet landing on the far side of the runway and turned to look. Though the rain had let up, the glare of the tower lights blurred everything with a fine haze. Still, they could all make out the Cyrillic lettering on the plane's side.

Celeste, recalling the security guards she'd overheard on the day—mere weeks ago—that she'd dropped Willow off at the airport, could not resist:

"Ooh, super, Clive!," she said in the voice of a squealing little girl. "Here come the bloody Rooskies!"

"Well," Elaine muttered. "Nature does abhor a vacuum."

"We got rid of some bad guys," Celeste reminded them as they squeezed water from their coats and climbed into Elaine's Mercedes. "We didn't get rid of the badness."

Elaine cranked the heater all the way up until Celeste could almost feel steam rising from her clothes. She ignored it, filling her friends in on the events leading up to the showdown.

"I've been thinking," said Abby when they were almost home. "Maybe we should join Human Rights Watch. Or Amnesty International."

"Really?" Elaine drawled.

Abby was brave. "Yes, why not? Like Celeste said, the evil's still out there."

"So you'll attend meetings and conferences?" asked Celeste. "You'll picket and protest? You'll travel to Third World countries, live in the rough, risk your personal safety, maybe get arrested?"

After a long moment, Abby said: "Well, at least we can give them some money."

Celeste and Elaine laughed. "That's what I thought," said Celeste.

Abby persisted. "A lot of money. Right?"

"Yes, we can. But there are other things we can do, things going on here. Neil says that forced prostitution has become big business in Moscow since the Soviet collapse. We know some important people now. We can ask pointed questions. Make a lot of noise. And help the girls tell their story to the world."

"Yes," Elaine said casually, pulling into Celeste's drive. "Just because we're not heroes doesn't mean we can't do something heroic."

Celeste grinned and got out of the car, then ducked her head back down, reaching in to squeeze their hands. "Cheers," she told her friends. "That's British for 'I'll see you soon.'"

EPILOGUE

In the full ripeness of afternoon, Keene stands alone addressing the flowerbeds. At first Celeste, uniquely tuned to his voice, thinks he's offering some kind of prayer, but as she draws near, she realizes he is reciting a poem:

"A garden is a lovesome thing, God wot!"

"Lovesome?" Celeste murmurs. And what on earth is a wot?

But Keene only continues:

"Rose plot,
Fringed pool,
Ferned grot—
The veriest school
Of peace; and yet the fool
Contends that God is not—
Not God! in gardens! when the eve is cool?
Nay, but I have a sign;
'Tis very sure God walks in mine."

"I'm going to go out on a limb here and assume you didn't make that up," she says when he stops.

Keene gives her a wry smile. "Afraid not. That was Thomas Edward Brown, 1830-1897. We had to memorize a poem in grammar school. I chose the shortest one I could find and somehow managed never to forget it."

"It sounded like you were blessing the garden."

"Did it?"

"I've heard there are no atheists in foxholes," Celeste says. "Maybe no atheists in flower beds either."

They both turn to contemplate the new garden, or rather gardens: four freshly dug beds, one for each girl to command —Celeste thought giving each her own would give them some much-needed autonomy. Besides, she rather likes the idea of the whole back yard converted to garden. Keene plans to lay stones for winding footpaths through the beds.

The girls have taken months, poring over seed catalogs, to choose their colors—Celeste's living room is stacked with garden dream-boards. Najima, unsurprisingly, chose all shades of pink: strawberry is still her favorite flavor. The other girls liked pink but also wanted purple, yellow, gold, blue, orange, scarlet. Celeste made four lists. Then she and Keene went shopping at local nurseries, buying seedlings so the girls wouldn't have to wait too long for blooms. It's going to be a backyard party, a gaudy hodgepodge of color.

Keene and Benny, wearing matching straw hats—a joke-gift from Celeste which they accepted with straight faces—dug the beds, adding compost and fertilizer, then showed the girls how to scoop out a hole, pour in a little water, shake the seedling out of its pot, loosen its roots, nestle it in its new home, cover with soil, then water again. The girls handle their plants gently and watch over them like mothers. Already, snapdragons, cornflowers, phlox, and sweet William are starting to bloom. Soon the buds of Michaelmas daisy, Canterbury bells, stock, freesia, and speedwell will open. Later there will be beardtongue, sneezewort, asters, heliotrope, and lilies. Just saying the names makes Celeste giddy.

Today, Fadeelah, Jameela, and Dafiyah are weeding and pinching back under Benny's supervision, while Keene tenderly installs his choicest dahlia tubers, so many variations, each a stunner in its own way. The girls have also requested flowers that attract butterflies and hummingbirds—something Keene has described with great enthusiasm—so next he plans to build trellises for sweet peas, trumpet vine, wisteria, morning glory. Beyond the garden walls, the city is packed with people in shorts and sunglasses, the sidewalks cluttered with little tables where customers sip cool frothy drinks. It seems that summer has come at last to England.

Arms full of baby, burp cloth, and blanket, Najima bumps the kitchen door open with her hip, a skill she's recently perfected. At first the intense sun recalls the glare of the desert, the wavy dunes and endless horizon, the pure sea of rippling sand. Then, as the baby stirs in her arms, she reminds herself that the desert wasn't all romantic billowy dunes. It was also hard gray gravel strewn with trash. That was the desert the slave trader drove her through. It is good, she decides, to remember both kinds of desert.

The baby utters a strangled protest, and blazing desert is instantly replaced by patches of rich naked earth, dots of color, green stems shooting up straight. Everyone turns to watch as Najima settles into her chair, but only she can hear the tiny grunts and lip-smacks as the baby searches for the nipple. Najima allows herself a moment to admire the velvety head, the suggestion of eyebrows, the pursing mouth. Then she gets down to business. The baby latches on, the milk flows, and Najima smiles, gazing down on the face of her daughter.

She'd been born here, at home. Myrtle the midwife saw no reason why not, and Celeste thought Najima wouldn't do as well in a hospital. Besides, there were so many eager helpers that they had to start a sign-up list to prevent clashes. The birth had gone smoothly—Najima sending a silent prayer of thanks to the fertility goddess whose broken bits she'd once bedecked with flowers—with Myrtle, Celeste, and Flora at her side and everyone else downstairs, straining to hear the baby's first cry. But what they heard instead was laughter.

When Myrtle lifted the glistening infant and the women saw what was—or rather, wasn't—between her legs, Celeste and Flora burst out laughing. When Najima caught her breath, she laughed too. Tariq's despised rival, Muhktar's embarrassment, Mehraj's envy, Ghassan's shame…and all along it was a mere girl, powerless, eligible to inherit nothing, claiming zero rights. Soon everyone was laughing, everyone understood the perfect irony.

Najima reached for the tiny girl, umbilical cord still connecting them, and murmured: "*Ahlan wa sahlan binti.*" Then she smiled at Celeste, whose eyes were brimming, and translated the words herself: "Welcome, daughter."

While Myrtle cleaned and swaddled the infant, Celeste, Flora, and Najima discussed names. Najima did not want to give her daughter an Arabic name. She wanted to call her "Celeste." But Celeste said one of her was enough, and Jews believed you should never name a child for a living person, because when the time came, the Angel of Death might confuse them and take the wrong soul. She suggested several pretty names. So did Myrtle and Flora.

But Najima wanted to honor Celeste. And she wanted a name that connected the baby to both of them—and, oddly, to Finsen as well: he had shown her it was possible to imagine a different universe. While Myrtle changed the bed sheets, Najima studied the framed print of *Starry, Starry Night* on the wall. She remembered the night they'd realized that Najima meant star and Celeste meant heaven, and, looking into her baby's calm midnight eyes, asked Flora for other names that meant star. Everyone liked Estella. Baby Stella. It was perfect. They placed the cradle below the print, and Najima rested, satisfied. Though she intended to teach her daughter their history, Stella would be a Western girl, free of the primitive bias that constricted the lives of Jadali females.

But she was not entirely surprised when, a few days later, she lifted the baby out of the cradle and discovered blue beads sewn to her Babygro. Blue to keep away the Evil Eye. She checked the other tiny garments: blue beads on each one. Probably Fadeelah's doing. Najima left the beads alone and said nothing. They'd all just survived a major brush with evil. The beads couldn't hurt. There were lots of Farouqis in the world.

Keene's sources have reported that Muhktar, who would not care to learn that he has a new daughter, has recovered from his bullet wound and returned to Jadal with his family—minus Tariq, who will be a guest of the British government for quite some time. Acutely aware of how Tariq betrayed him, the family, and The Judgments, Muhktar disowned his only son. He put *Hadiqa House* on the market, transferred his treasures to the new Jadali Royal Museum, and forbade Tariq's name ever to be mentioned in his presence. Luckily, Mehraj is pregnant again, this time surely with a new son and heir. Begum lives in her suite, alone except for her servants. Muhktar, soothed by his 16th century Safavid carpets and Qajar tapestries, his rooms fragrant with rosewater, has turned his attention to a lucrative new project: the construction of The Jewel of Jadal shopping mall, filling it with choking perfume, a three-story fountain, expensive golden light, and female mannequins with no faces.

Stella utters a tiny sigh and drops the nipple, mouth curling in the goofy smile that signals the end of a fine meal. With fingers made nimble from practice, Najima refastens the baby's sunbonnet, pausing to admire her pink pomegranate cheeks. Her heart swells against her ribs as if it's grown too big for her chest.

"Burp time?" asks Celeste, holding out her arms.

Najima grins, handing the baby over. From Celeste's expression, you'd think she's just been awarded every treasure in the Royal Museum. Though she's never had a child of her own, she seems to know instinctively how to sway, pat, and murmur. When she manages to extract a respectable burp, she beams. Flora comes over to have a look. Then Benny. Then Keene.

Najima takes advantage of the break to join the other girls watering their seedlings and practicing English conversation. Everyone speaks a few words of English now, Najima most of all. Celeste has provided them with headphones, CD players, and a home course in Arabic-to-English, so each girl can progress at her own pace. They practice diligently every day. Celeste herself practices English-to-Arabic lessons. Soon they will all start taking classes. And meanwhile, television is a great teacher: Fadeelah has proven exceptionally adept at reproducing cakes made on baking shows and adding her own twists. Jameela and Dafiyah make good sous chefs. The girls' dream is to open a bakery together, maybe with a flat above where they could live. This plan was actually Celeste's idea: Abby, Elaine, and Willow are prevailing upon their husbands to provide interest-free loans. And Willow is establishing a non-profit foundation to help disadvantaged women start their own businesses in Britain. The girls will be among her first clients. Already they're learning about publicity and branding and business plans, about offering free tastings, about selling their goods on commission to build up clientele. Excited, they chatter about the great plan, slipping into Arabic, gently nudging each other back to English. For the first time ever, they can imagine being free and equal in this strange new society.

Meanwhile, the husbands, Keene, and Willow are pulling every string they can to get the girls' status normalized. It looks like the Home Office will grant asylum since a return to Jadal would indeed entail a "well-founded fear of persecution" and "reasonable risk of serious harm," namely death by honor-killing. From there they can pursue the path to citizenship: the girls were surprised and pleased to learn that a woman sits on the throne of their new country. And Celeste has already been awarded temporary guardianship of Najima, who has just turned sixteen.

But Celeste has bigger plans than that. She's begun exploring the adoption process. Najima will need years of schooling before she can tackle college; meanwhile, Celeste will have both a baby and a teenager to raise. She watches as Flora takes a turn with Stella, Benny and Keene offering fingers for the baby to grip and realizes that this child will have two sets of grandparents after all, as well as some very cool aunts. How has life managed to become so much bigger and so much smaller at the same time?

The girls discuss the baby's progress, their English lessons, and Shorsh Ka-loon-ee: it turns out that Dafiyah and Jameela love ER just as much as everyone else. Najima can understand some of the dialogue now. It occurs to her, when she watches the young doctors race down the corridor, white coats flapping, that they are like desert warriors galloping in their robes, except that these people save people.

Next the girls discuss their newest baking experiment—bouquets of cupcakes designed to look like flowers. Already they've perfected one that looks like the pink speckled lilies Keene first brought them, the stargazers. They decide that the stargazer cupcakes will be their new business logo—they take turns repeating this important new word—because a logo is good marketing strategy. They nod wisely at each other. But when Fadeelah adds: *"Inshallah"*—if God wills it—Najima does not chime in agreement with the others.

"I don't think everything that happens is God's will," she says instead. "I think every human soul contains a garden with a snake who whispers. Men like Tariq, women like Begum, they choose to listen."

Fadeelah is shocked. "But how could God make a universe in which something is against his will?"

Najima replies with a little smile: "I'm not sure. But Celeste says not sure is an interesting place to be." When the others stare blankly, she explains: "It's something every person has to work out for herself." She almost adds: Like the blue beads, then doesn't.

But she gets unexpected support from Jameela, tiny timid Jameela, who says slowly, as if fearing a lightning bolt: "The Judgments say that all men are equal before God. If that is true, how can some buy and sell others?"

No one can answer. Not yet.

Celeste and Keene observe the girls' serious faces but understand little until Flora translates the conversation. Flora is jiggling the baby, who, despite a full stomach and clean nappy, seems loath to settle down—one little fist batters the air as if seeking an opponent.

"A right pugilist, that one," Benny observes proudly.

Flora shushes, rocks, and bobs, finally handing the baby to Celeste. "You have a go. I've got to get the tea." She gives the padded bottom one last pat. "Proper tea today? Or lemonade again?"

"Oh, the girls can't get enough of your lemonade," said Celeste. "Especially when it's pink."

Flora hides a pleased smile—making the lemonade pink had been her idea—then bustles inside to see about refreshments.

Stella, displaying impressive baby-power, is still making little grunts of protest and thrashing her legs. Now it's Celeste's turn to swivel, jiggle, and pat. She even tries blowing softly across the baby's face, something her own grandmother used to do—"to blow away evil spirits," her father always joked, only it wasn't entirely a joke. Nothing works. But when Keene lowers his large face to the tiny one, the baby hiccups and hushes, fixing him with her stern gaze. Celeste needs no further encouragement: she thrusts the baby at Keene, admiring the ease with which he cradles her one-handed, like a football. An American football.

With the baby settled, Celeste turns to check on the girls again. They're no longer chattering. Each seems lost in thought.

"They're contemplating big questions," she says softly to Keene, "and they aren't used to thinking for themselves. They were talking about free agency just now: the power of the individual." Then she repeats the proverb Tariq cited while conducting her tour of *Hadiqa House*: "*I against my brother. I and my brother against my cousins. I and my cousins against my tribe. I and my tribe against the world.*"

"He should have just said I and myself against everyone else and left it at that," Keene adds dryly.

She nods. "I don't think I'm naïve or particularly idealistic. But I just don't get it."

"What?"

"The hate." She bends to scoop a fistful of fresh earth, letting it sift through her fingers. "Even plain callousness is a passive form of hate, don't you think? Such contempt: Tariq, Begum, the terrorists, the traffickers denying the autonomy of every human soul."

"I've spent my entire adult life in law enforcement," says Keene. "I've seen acts of cruelty that would curdle milk. And I don't get it either, not really."

"A rotten apple or two I could understand. But whole institutions—education, religion, government, cultural identity —that teach hate, reinforce it." She looks at him. "It's arbitrary. It's absurd. Why don't they see it?"

Keene is delivered from having to answer an unanswerable question by Flora's return with a tray of gingersnaps and lemonade. The girls look up, pulling off their gardening gloves. Keene, still one-handed, manages to snag three cookies, giving one to Celeste and keeping two for himself, having learned from painful experience that if he does not take seconds now, there will be nothing left when the tray comes back.

His ears pink up when he sees her watching. "Excellent biscuits," he mumbles through the crumbs on his lips.

Celeste grins. "Why do Brits call cookies biscuits?" she asks, reviving their old game.

"Because we were here first," says Keene. "So that's their name."

"And why call sweaters jumpers? Does a jumper jump?"

"Does a sweater sweat?"

"And this"—she touches the baby's ruffled cap—"is a bonnet. The front of the car is called a hood."

"And the back is called a boot," he counters again.

Now they're both laughing.

"And perhaps we ought to discuss correct usage of the word *pudding*," says Celeste.

"That one's easy. Pudding is the best part of a meal." He tugs out a handkerchief to wipe his mouth. "Just the thing after a chip buddy—what you lot would call French fries on buttered bread."

"No!" Celeste pretends to be shocked. "Who would eat that?"

"Or boiled potato topped with canned corn and cream. Delicious."

"No!" she says again, genuinely horrified, then studies his expression. "Oh. You're kidding."

"No," he says, using the handkerchief to dab a pink drop from her lips. "I'm having you on."

"Maybe I should sign you up for English classes along with the girls."

"My English is perfect. Now classes in American might be useful."

And so the game continues. As if reminding them that the world is not an entirely benign place, Keene's phone buzzes periodically with reports from the detectives he's supervising. Every call represents some evil, some human pain. Keene's face goes still when he takes these calls, tempting Celeste to seize his phone and bury it deep in the garden. Give the man some peace. But that's like closing your eyes—it solves nothing. Good and evil: the old, old story. Maybe the only story, when you came right down to it.

Still, she can't help feeling victorious, gazing out at her

lovesome plot: the girls tending their flowers, Flora tending the girls, baby Stella finally asleep, Benny and Keene keeping watch over all. And she can't help making a wish—*God wot*—upon stars she can't see but knows are there, that this peace will last forever.

Then she has to laugh at her own temerity: why ask for the impossible? It's enough that they are all here now, whole and safe and together. It's enough that baby, girls, and seedlings all flourish, that the light of the late afternoon seems endless, that summer has only just begun. Tipping back her head, she closes her eyes and lets the warmth of the English sun push through her veins like slow honey.

UPCOMING FROM
PALM BEACH PRESS

(novels)

SKYCLAD ON BOURBON STREET by Carol K. Howell, is a contemporary tale about Jewish witches in New Orleans that blends realism with magic.

THE UNBELIEVABLE TALE by Carol K. Howell, is the story of Ivy Perlman, a burned-out college professor in a dead-end job looking for a way out; she encounters a psychic, a murder, and a mysterious search for the truth of the Nazi camps.

WINGS OF MADNESS by Sheila Hollihan-Elliot and Carol K. Howell, is a fictionalized biography of Gilded Age artist Abbott Handerson Thayer.

(novellas)

THE MAGICIAN OF BROOKLYN by Carol K. Howell, inspired by Isaac Bashevis Singer's THE MAGICIAN OF LUBLIN, is a contemporary tale of a young Hasidic woman in Williamsburg who dreams of being a singer, something forbidden to Hasidic women.

THE EMPTY BOWL by Carol K. Howell, tells the story of a young German woman working as a secretary in a death camp much like Auschwitz.

HAVDALAH, by Carol K. Howell, which references a ritual conducted by observant Jews at the end of each Sabbath, pairs Michaela, a cynical young woman and child of Holocaust survivors, with Eli, a young veteran of the Israeli wars who is suffering PTSD.

(story collections)

THE HAPPY SAPPERSTEINS by Carol K. Howell, linked stories about a functioning dysfunctional Jewish-American Family. (REDEMPTION is one of the stories, published in 2020 as a Kindle e-book.)

GITTEL'S GOLEM AND OTHER STORIES OF MAGIC REALISM, by Carol K. Howell, includes award winning stories Gittel's Golem, The Demon's Debut, Mrs. Cohen's Conversion, and more.

ABOUT THE AUTHOR

Carol K. Howell

Carol K. Howell, a 1985 graduate of the Iowa Writers' Workshop, has published over 60 stories in literary magazines and anthologies, including Epoch, New Orleans Review, Story/Quarterly, The North American Review, and Crazyhorse, written two novels on her own--one about Jewish witches in New Orleans and another about psychics and the Holocaust, and 3 novellas --as well as 3 new novels with her collaborator, Sheila Hollihan-Elliot. After spending 30 years teaching college writing courses, she now leads public workshops and provides coaching and editing for individual writers. A trained dramatist and speaker, she is available for readings, book club online programs, and conference events.

ABOUT THE AUTHOR

Sheila Hollihan-Elliot

Sheila Elliot, represented by her 7-year-old avatar, writes primarily under the name Sheila Hollihan-Elliot. Previously an award-winning documentary film writer and non-fiction book author, she is now senior editor of the regional Hook Magazine www.TheHook.org. She's lately been collaborating with author Carol K.  Howell on several fiction novels - Wings of Madness: about Gilded Age artist Abbott Handerson Thayer; Traffik Games, a suspense novel exploring the current practice of human slavery; and a new project revealing the legacies of 20th C artist Marc Chagall. She is creating a micro-publishing company Palm Beach Press Inc., believing that the 21st C place to publish books is on the internet. Her key areas of interest are Art & Artists, Art History, Chinese Studies - and cats! www.sheilaelliot.com www.thepalmbeachpress.com sheilahollihanelliot@gmail.com

BOOK CLUB QUESTIONS

*** (1) Choose one of these patterns or motifs and trace its development throughout the story. What purpose(s) does it serve beyond mere description?

a.   Imagery of gardens, flowers, fertility, snakes
b.   Imagery of weather, stars, heavens
c.   Color imagery, especially pink
d.   Games motif
e.   Food motif
f.   Language motif

*** (2) What role do religious/philosophical beliefs play in the story? How do the authors reconcile these different beliefs? What message do they ultimately suggest?

*** (3) What do you make of this sentence, uttered once by Celeste before they storm the hospital and once by Elaine at the very end: *Just because we're not heroes doesn't mean we can't do something heroic.* How are or aren't the women heroes? Why does it matter?

*** (4) Make a list of adjectives that describe Celeste or Najima or Flora. What are the authors trying to suggest about these characters? Why?

*** (5) What do you make of Abby's suggestion, in chapter 12, that the women join a human rights group? Why do her friends react the way they do?

*** (6) Consider the personalities of the major characters. How would you describe each one? What important purpose(s) do their personalities and relationships serve besides providing

information? How does their connection to one another reflect
the themes of the novel?

NGO'S TO CONTACT

https://www.dhs.gov/dhs-center-countering-human-trafficking
USA Department of Homeland Security multilevel official outreach and training how to recognize and combat human trafficking

http://www.endslaverynow.org/about/volunteer-with-us
End Slavery Now believes we all have a role in ending slavery. We try to illustrate the many different ways normal, everyday individuals can get involved in the fight.

https://www.unodc.org/unodc/en/human-trafficking/index.html
United Nations offers programs, partnerships and e-learning for civil society to combat human trafficking.

https://www.state.gov/20-ways-you-can-help-fight-human-trafficking/
USA Department of State guidance of organizations you can contact and how to volunteer to help stop human trafficking.

5 Ways for You to Help Stop Human Trafficking Right Now
- Raise awareness. The problem will not end unless everyone knows it's there in the first place. ...
- Fundraise for anti-trafficking organizations. ...
- Volunteer for anti-trafficking organizations. ...
- Civic engagement: promote anti-trafficking legislation. ...
- Reporting human trafficking.

www.ingramcontent.com/pod-product-compliance
Lightning Source LLC
Chambersburg PA
CBHW072011170726
47999CB00014B/1520